AF080755

OLIVIA BELL

BLUEROSE PUBLISHERS
India | U.K.

Copyright © Olivia Bell 2024

All rights reserved by author. No part of this publication may be reproduced, stored in a retrieval system or transmitted in any form or by any means, electronic, mechanical, photocopying, recording or otherwise, without the prior permission of the author. Although every precaution has been taken to verify the accuracy of the information contained herein, the publisher assumes no responsibility for any errors or omissions. No liability is assumed for damages that may result from the use of information contained within.

BlueRose Publishers takes no responsibility for any damages, losses, or liabilities that may arise from the use or misuse of the information, products, or services provided in this publication.

For permissions requests or inquiries regarding this publication, please contact:

BLUEROSE PUBLISHERS
www.BlueRoseONE.com
info@bluerosepublishers.com
+91 8882 898 898
+4407342408967

ISBN: 978-93-6452-891-7

Cover Design: Sadhna Kumari
Typesetting: Pooja Sharma

First Edition: September 2024

To the people who think weird things keep happening to them.

you are not alone; we are on the same ship...

Disclaimer

This is a work of fiction. Names, characters, places, and events are either the product of the author's imagination or used fictitiously. Any resemblance to actual persons, living or dead, or to real events is purely coincidental.

The Right Path

Why do we enjoy and why do we laugh
If we have to part, then why do we start?

Experiences are meant to be fleeting
There is nothing permanent
There is nothing perfect

Keep connecting the tiny dots
After all, oceans are made of tiny drops

Don't cry that it's over,
But smile that it happened

Sky is the limit
Yet it has no end

Sky is a limit
Take the right start and
you will be remembered forever in the end

Chapter 1

"A ship is always safe at the shore, but that is not what it is built for." -*Albert Einstein.*

I don't think I hate it. Wherever you go you must give yourself a chance to try new things. Especially when you want to grow and explore the world.

"I'm starting to hate this place more with every passing minute." Says Jane. It's not as bad as I thought it would be.

"We have been here for not more than a day; you better wait before making decisions"

The words were out before I decided on actually saying them. but I am not sure what would be a better way to make her accept the fact that we have 10 more months to survive here. I am sitting on my bed facing her. She has straight long black hair (keratin treatment offcourse), black cat eyes and flawless skin.

Its Sunday evening.

"Come on, it's time for the movie" Blair, my senior comes into our room ~~her room~~ to take us for the movie in the auditorium. movie? I have never heard of a boarding school like this.

After the movie ended, we headed to the dining hall for dinner which is about a mile away. Grace comes to the table waving her hand like we have known each other for years rather than days.

"So, how was the day?" she asked me. Sitting right beside me and Jane.

"I hate the fact that today I was supposed to enjoy our festival with my family but I was also not willing to skip my first day here so, here I am complaining about unnecessary things and trying hard to be strong as I'm away from my parents for the first time" I finish and look at her face that has a glimpse of shock at my too honest reply.

"It's fine, you'll get used to this place eventually." She says politely and continues to eat. Another 'seniorie' assumption.

Our dinner is done. I try to finish unpacking within the next 2 hours. I arrange everything in the wardrobe which is half of the size compared to the one I have at home. Little less than half to be precise.

The furniture is good, everything is made of marble, only the wardrobe has wooden doors. Luckily, there are 8 washrooms in total and 7 people on our floor so, everyone has their personal one.

I'm done with my sheets and now I am sitting on the corner of my bed when I notice one of my seniors looking sick and lying helpless in her bed, across to me.

"Hey, do you need any help?" As I asked her, she gave me a sweet smile and spoke

"Once you get used to this place, you'll get tired to ask for help" she smiled.

I don't even know her name till now but, I feel bad for her. WHY is everyone here sick of this place?

"Have you eaten anything Raquel?" Blair comes into the room with a box of chocolate biscuits, asking the sick person on bed. I believed packaged food is not allowed here. They might have some tricks to it though.

Every room is on four sharing basis. I share the room with Blair and Raquel who are my seniors, and there is Jane. She is in the same class as me and just moved in today.

Moving in is not an appropriate word to use but it suits our situation as we brought all our stuff which will be enough for calling this place a home.

Me and Jane are listening to how the things work here as Sarah and Grace are helping us with the schedule. Blair joins us and now all of them are scaring us about the hectic schedule. Sarah is sitting on my study table beside my bed, others are all sitting on my bed whereas I am sitting in the corner.

It feels good to have people like them around. When I saw Grace for the first time, short blond wavy hair, hooded hazel eyes, and a face girls would kill for. I thought she might be full of herself and I still am unsure.

On the other hand, Sarah is good to talk with unless she starts acting full of herself, tallest girl in the campus, flawless skin, light brown bangs touching her brows and sharp blue eyes.

It looks like Blair and Raquel are not on good terms. They barely spoke throughout the day. I think I will get to know a lot of drama after a few days.

"Where are the new girls who ca…" someone enters the room asking about us I think, and stops in the middle of completing her sentence when she sees all of us sitting together and having a good time. Long black hair just like her charcoal black eyes. Something about her nose bothers me though.

"Oh, Linda the flat nose is here" just as I heard Blair growl at her, she does in fact have a flat nose.

It's quite funny but I think it's better to control my laughter at this point. As soon as she enters, everyone starts to leave.

More drama.

I don't think she is someone they hate but it's best if I don't start judging people this early. Jane is now sitting on her study table beside her bed, writing about her day. Both of us are now in our comfy night suits.

It's me and Linda sitting together now as she is sharing some of her experiences with me. When she told me it's been 8 years since she's been here. A thought occurred to me, "even the insects here would know you" but I kept it to myself.

Linda went after wasting my 2 precious hours and now I'm writing about my day to my mom and Rose.

Rose and I have been together for the past 7 years in which we made a bond no one would have imagined, including ourselves. After I'm done writing to them, I start with my journaling which I think I'll be maintaining throughout the year.

Well, that's what I hope for.

Chapter 2

*I*t's been a week since we {the whole new class 11th} were welcomed in the assembly. Many things have happened in my first week.

I showed my harry potter socks in the class to the teacher who is crazy for fictional characters and he was already discussing harry potter in the class, it was my most embarrassing moment in the class until it wasn't.

I tripped while playing with on one of my classmates on the basketball court and I don't know why but it turned out to be the person I am most afraid to talk to. Tall, dark hair, sportsmen personality and his mysterious light brown eyes, always carrying a disgusted and intimidating look on his face.

We had art classes every week which was my most refjuvenating class. I hated the teacher though as he never provided me with the supplies I needed but, eventually things were going just fine. I started hating him a little less, comparatively.

I'm standing in front of a pottery table right now. I have my clay in front of me and I don't think I'm good at this stuff.

I just started with the wedging process but as soon as one of my classmates saw me, he started laughing at me.

"What now?" my question made him flinch. I guess he was not supposed to react out loud. He is wearing a brown mud coloured shirt with cream pants. This guy doesn't even know how to wear clothes and here he is, laughing at me?

"You are doing it wrong" as he said that, he is hurting my ears with his donkey like voice. His hair looks like someone has given him an electric shock. His name is Jay, as far as I remember from our introductory session in the assembly hall yesterday.

"You are doing even worse" Here comes Mr. Pedrot the teacher who made me hate him a little more less as this was the first time, I heard him saying something more suitable.

The guy has now stopped laughing. I have my hands already covered in clay but I cannot afford to get my watch dirty. I handed my watch to Ethan, the scary looking guy from basketball. He has been in the school for the last 2 years.

He is the only person who I think has a brain unlike the rest of the class. He is keeping my watch on a shelf which has a lot of dust. The pottery room has shelves all over the walls and a long table with a marble top in the middle which is being used by us.

"don't keep it there" I said as I hated my things getting dirty.

He gives me an annoying look and asks "why?"

"Because it has dust all over it"

"Then lick it" he laughs...

A moment of awkward silence and there he goes proving me wrong.

I was just hoping one of my classmates might have a little bit of sense. I was proved wrong. I can understand not everyone can afford a well-functioning brain but why does it have to be me stuck between this bunch of nut shells? I make a face and here he goes again

"Why are you making a lady-like face?" he raised one eye brow.

Before I could say anything, Jay said "she is a lady so she'll obviously make a lady face, not gentlemen face"

Now I'm out of words and they are laughing like a psycho. I don't have words for them...

I just don't.

*****

After a few days the whole school went to a tree plantation on the hills by foot and it was fun. Everyone had their personalized name tags to indicate the trees they planted. We have been practicing for the freshers' day since last week, our whole class consists of freshers except Ethan and Trevor. Jane is good at dancing so she took 5 other classmates of ours for the dance.

A new guy joined us today while the practice is going on. By looking at his face I feel he is a creep. His name is Mateo and he is weird just like his name. Joint eyebrows, small brown guy.

Whenever he tries to talk to me, I find myself shouting at him or getting angry for no reason. Jay is the only person keeping him away from me because he knows if I lose my temper on him, I might end up having his blood on my hands.

While I am sitting with Jay, preparing for our anchoring. I can see Jane and Mateo fighting. I am completely devoted to anchoring and public speaking activities when it comes to school events. Dancing and singing are not my cup of tea.

"Who the hell are you to teach me?" Jane is now yelling at him. Standing right in the middle of the assembly hall with other freshers catching her attention.

"And who are you to yell at me?" he also started yelling at her.

"Don't act like a know it all, you know nothing about dance" Jane scoffs.

"You want it to be this way? Fine! I'll show you what real dance is. Just wait and watch." Mateo starts to stomp off.

"Come on people! Finish it already, we are no more interested in this. We are leaving" and now others have started to leave as they are no longer listening to the dance leaders.

Me and Jay are enjoying the drama though. We are nearly done with our script and that's when someone comes yelling my name.

Oh crap!

Chapter 3

"How could you forget about making the program sequence?"

Oh right, Mr. Danial told me to make *that* list last Sunday while every coordinating teacher was present in the assembly hall for the practice.

"I'm so sorry sir, we will go immediately to the teachers and start the work on it" I try my best to sound sincere.

"There's no need for that now, I have already done that work" that's when I realize he is holding a bunch of papers with a notebook.

"Now listen to me carefully both of you, you will be the host and will be concluding the program too. I have taken the necessary information. You guys just must arrange the order according to your anchoring. I need it prepared till tomorrow and if any changes are required, I'll let you know." He finishes.

It's not much, we'll be fine with this or at least that's what I hope for, Mr. Danial called everyone from our class and now all of us are sitting in a big circle. It's the second time all of us are sitting together since I came here.

It feels like I have known these people for a long time but I don't even remember most of their names till now.

The freak is now explaining his dance steps to the group but as a matter of fact no one is interested in his rubbish. When he first introduced himself to the group, I laughed the way he pronounced his name. That day he never asked me my name but after the practice he was *following* me and Jane to our Dormitory.

"Do you wanna go to the girls' hostel?" I said that sarcastically but, what he said made me almost punch him in the face.

"If you get me the entry I'll come" he smirked. what the hell is wrong with this guy?

I was about to punch him at the time but Jay jumped in between and dragged him to the side of the boy's dormitory saying "Are you crazy man? She'll kill you if you mess with her"

That day he was saved but if he does something like that again, I won't just joke about whatever I was thinking to do to him.

We are being called for practice daily during the sports time. I don't *miss* sports though because half of the population here is enrolled in badminton so, I don't like to play in front of many people as I'm not good at it.

In the morning, Mr. Aden, our class teacher took most of our classes as he was in a hurry to complete the syllabus. It's been more than a week since I've been staying and observing this place but it's not as bad as I thought it would be.

The food here is my only problem though as I'm not a vegan. I do enjoy each movement here as it's my first-time experiencing residential school life. The teachers are very friendly and easy to approach, almost everyone. The environment is green and clean.

It feels like you are on a vacation and staying at a hill station. The infrastructure is built in such a way that the classes look like cottages and they are built with stones and everything is Eco friendly.

We get all the facilities here like, laundry goes two times a week and the clothes are ironed before being returned. We get a tuck list twice a week in which we can write the necessary things required and when we submit the list our stuff is prepared and handed over in the next three days. There are two doctors. They are the couple who are available 24/7 for us. They live in the campus itself behind the dining hall. They also have an isolation ward for keeping injured or sick cases.

"Where is Olivia?" Mr. Aden asked for me in the assembly hall now and I was lost in my thoughts. When I reach him, I can tell by the look on his face that he has already asked more than 20 people for me.

"Follow me to the staff room, we have a lot of work to do." I am curious what work made him come and get me himself. Passing the art block we reach the staff room.

When we are in the staff room, I see Ethan and Trevor using the computers and they are searching something on YouTube? Using computers all without supervision? Now that looks like important work.

Chapter 4

The rule is strict. No electronic gadgets allowed in the campus for students. Except computers in supervision. I am standing behind Ethans' chair as he is facing the computer. Trevor is on his right and Mr. Aden is on his left.

"Sit here and tell me what are you going to sing"

wait... what?

"Are you joking?" this must be a joke.

"Are you crazy?" he sounds serious.

"You are the crazy one here Ethan. What, why and how am I supposed to sing?" I try not to panic.

"Oh right, I thought you could use the same vocal cord for singing which you use to pass silly comments" he is mocking me.

"I'm being serious" I am.

"So, you really have a different vocal cord to sing? Wow that is creepy" he shudders.

This guy is getting on my nerves now.

"Just shut up you two and focus on the work" Trevor interrupts our talk which was turning into an argument.

"Get to the point Trevor, what's with the singing? You guys are freaking me out" I am freaking out.

"We are performing a rain assembly next week and you have to sing a song on rain" says Trevor. The skinniest and the smartest guy in our batch who is also a jerk and never spoke to me before until now. He is *ordering* me to sing.

I'm trying to process what he just said. Do they seriously want me to sing? And in the assembly?

"I cannot do it, just give me the anchoring part"

Please. Now I am scared.

"I have already prepared the anchoring for me and Jane, you are the one left and that's the only activity left for you" Trevor says not even looking at me from his computer.

"Does Jane know? Has she agreed?" I am still hoping for a chance that I know I will never get.

"Doesn't matter because she doesn't have a choice. But you can take Denise with you if you want" He suggests, now looking at me.

oh yes, there is a girl named Denise in our class. Long curly black hair, THE TOPPER of our class. I haven't talked to her much because she is in science and she doesn't live with us because she is the principal's daughter. Now that I don't have any other option, I think it might be fine if we just sing together but the thing is how will we practice for it.

"You can ask her to come at your dorm for practice if you want" Trevor answers my un-asked question.

"Is it fine?" Really?

"As long as she is willing to cooperate" Ethan shrugs.

I don't think she will say no. I will just go to her after I'm free from here.

"You can sing 'raindrops keep falling on my head' by B.J. Thomas. It's easy and it will work fine for our purpose" Mr. Aden suggested to me the song and now he is giving me the printouts for me and Denise to learn and practice. Now that my work here is done, I'm heading out of the staff room before I pause to ask Ethan what he is doing in the assembly.

"I'm learning a dialog by a famous actor which is about rain"

He doesn't elaborate, but I'm still thinking what he meant by 'learning.' Whatever, I just start to leave to find Denise and there is someone calling me. I'm standing in front of the admin office when the operator calls me to take my parcel. It's from mom.

Looks big enough to cover half of my body when I carry it but as I have no time to go back to the hostel to keep it and if I don't take it now, I'll have to wait until tomorrow so I'll just take it to the assembly hall. Just after I thought that, it started raining.

Now how am I supposed to carry this cardboard box half of my size along with an umbrella?

After struggling a little, I'm halfway there to the assembly hall. My hand starts slipping from the box. I see someone running in the rain to help me but before they come, I'm already in the shade.

"Need some help?" He asked.

Wow, you're early. That's what I wanted to say but anyways

"I'm fine"

what was his name again? I don't have time for that but at least I know he is my senior, scary one.

I am now standing in front of Jay and Mr. Danial watching how Jay is getting scolded. I laugh at him then out of nowhere Mr. Danial starts to scold me too. He is explaining to us how to react on which part and where to take a pause and when to continue. This is exhausting.

It's been a few days and now tomorrow we have our rain assembly. First activity our class will be performing.

Everyone is preparing themselves for tomorrow as there should be no mistakes. Trevor and Jane are sitting in their places, Ethan is walking round and round around the class reading his dialogue loudly.

Meanwhile, I and Denise are singing/screaming to learn the song. Then comes Mr. Aden, he tells me and Jane to collect all the umbrellas by tomorrow morning from all the girls and teachers whereas he tells the boys to collect the umbrellas from the rest of the population.

*****

As the day to our first assembly is here, we are taking all the umbrellas to the admin block as we collected them yesterday night. While me and Jane reach there we see Ethan, Trevor and Cyrus are already hanging the umbrellas they brought on the hooks all over the place.

After Denise is here, we do a run through and we all go back to get ready as all of us were in our night suits. The assembly was a success and now we have a bigger challenge coming up. Which is,

Freshers Day.

Chapter 5

Me and Jay have been working on the anchoring part well. Whenever we are in the staff room with Mr. Danial, all three of us are laughing half of the time while preparing the script.

It is fun to work with them but the fun has come to an end as the fresher's day is tomorrow.

Many things have happened since then, I'm trying to cooperate with that freaky Mateo, Jane has decided to perform a classical solo dance while Mateo is performing a pop solo.

Now I feel as if I am getting used to this place and the people. Feels like I am accepting how things work and I am more comfortable now as compared to the time I first came.

I used to get irritated very easily by anything as small as a bug on my bed but now I'm calmer and I take things easy. I have learned many new basic things like washing clothes as there is a limit for school laundry and I still am learning things on my own.

There are two pairs for anchoring, me and Jay were the main anchors whereas Rose and Henry are there for a few parts. The 'Rose' here is different from the Rose I wrote a letter to. I wrote a letter to Rose Williams who is a friend of mine from the past 7 years. If there is someone who knows me as well as my parents, it's Rose William. My other half.

The Rose who is with me now is Rose Tate. She is one of my juniors. She is jolly natured and she is the only one I feel like anchoring with other than Jay.

All of us spend most of our time after classes in the staffroom.

That's always the most stress relieving part of the day. Also, me and Jay went to the Chairmans' office with a program invitation card made specially by the art department for Freshers Day.

Me and Jay are sitting in the assembly hall and it's already evening. We have been revising the script throughout the day and now that we are finalizing our script according to the programs here comes another teacher.

He has worked in a few local television series and he is called in the school for organizing big events. He is now doing the last thing I expected him to do which is that he is changing our script.

Not just a little but, he changes the whole sequence upside down and it's a mixture of the previous performances along with some new ones added by him just now.

This is crazy! I can't work like this.

I mean the event is supposed to be tomorrow and he is creating a mess right now.

"I'm not gonna work like this" as I say irritatingly, I got something which I wasn't expecting.

"It's fine, we'll go and get someone else" he snaps at me.

What is wrong with this man? Is he crazy? Who is going to agree at the last movement to learn this scrap? He would have showed up early and we would not have wasted our energy on this scrap.

"Go and get whoever you want yourself, there is no chance I'm going to waste my time for your sake" This is what I wanted to say on his face but instead I said "I'll be the one doing it until you let me make the sequence myself including the new performances"

"Sure, just let me know before you finalize anything"

Mr. Scott leaves just like that.

What? Just like that? I thought he would argue more and I'll end up not doing it. Is this man for real? Tomorrow is Freshers Day and he still wants me to cross check with him for the sequence.

After the hard work and the efforts, me and Jay made in the last 3 hours, we finally finished the script and showed it to that man. He is okay with the script for *now* at least.

Me and Jay took our copies to learn it through the night. I practiced the script for at least 6 to 7 times as there was not much to learn because we just shuffled our content a little and most of it is the same, just some new unnecessary editions are done.

The night is rough. Whenever there is an event coming up, I would stay up all night and thanks to the unnecessary excitement popping in my head. I remember I received a letter from my mom two days ago which I haven't replied to till now.

When I kept my pen down to pack the letter there was a knock on the door to my room. When the person standing on the other side opens the door, I see what I was not expecting for the next few days.

Chapter 6

It's been a week since I rocked on Freshers Day. It was a success thanks to me covering up at the last movement announcements.

Jay had a stage fear so he was pushing me forward every time something new came up. Mateo stole the show as he is funny at dancing. Literally funny.

People were screaming for him to perform more. That was the only performance which was repeated thrice on public demand.

I became popular for mimicking because I called Mateo on the stage in the same funny way, he introduced himself on the very first day. That was not even the last thing I wanted to be popular for but it was so hilarious for the audience that it made everyone laugh hard. Seeing everyone laugh made me laugh.

I really enjoyed my first event and my first experience was amazing. I received two letters the night before freshers' day – one from my friends who I rarely talk too and the other one was from Rose, Rose Williams.

Everything is going great but there is still something bothering me. It is Sunday and there is no sun. That means a rainy day. Sundays are generally my most favourite and simultaneously most torturing days for me.

Every Sunday songs are played all over the campus. When the songs of my choice are being played in the dorm it's an amazing feeling to wait for a week to listen your songs but when the track changes, it's a torture for me.

I can't bare slow classical torture especially when you wait for a week to listen your songs and what you get is complete mental torture.

My tortures are enjoyable for some and some suffer just like me. It's not like kids enjoy me suffering through headache but people have different tastes so some enjoy the slow songs as well.

But when it comes to friends like Jane and Linda, they intentionally enjoy my pain. They sing the most torturing songs along in a loud voice that I have no choice but to leave the room. Wherever I go Jane follows me and sings for her enjoyment at my cost.

The worst part is when any song for the peace of my soul is being played and I rush to the bathroom so that I can take a peaceful bath, as always, the song track takes a horrible turn.

Jane always tells me that I should just skip the Sunday baths for the sake of my mental peace. Sometimes I thought it might help but anyways I just leave the dorm after taking the bath. I carry a novel or something to study with me and sit on the stairs in front of my class or else I just sleep. In my room obviously.

Sundays are boring as we don't have a schedule. I still remember the Sunday I joined. Climbing the stairs to first floor. My Dorm is a simple two floor building in a slight rectangle shape but hollow in the middle. Trees from the ground floor porch touching my floors' balcony railing.

I am allotted the second wing which had two occupied compartments on the back side of the room. The other two empty compartments on the front were allotted to me and Jane. I got the one on the left corner.

There are bed numbers written on every bed in the room, mine is 2. It means 2nd compartment. Pink curtains and pink walls, too girly.

I do my laundry every Sunday and I clean my compartment too. That's the only day I get the time to do other things. Though there is a laundry facility, the other reason I prefer to wash my favourite clothes myself is that if something happens to my clothes, I will be the one to blame.

There is also something that keeps my excitement for Sunday and that is the chilly garlic paste. It's made only on Sundays. The food here is close to tasteless and unfortunately, I am a foodie person. I love spicy food. There were times I thought I can't survive if I don't get spicy food. Now here I am eating nearly tasteless food just to survive.

I eagerly wait for the chilly garlic paste and I devour the meal as if I had been starving myself to death for the whole week. In short, I fill myself completely on Sundays so that it won't matter if I starve myself for the next whole week.

If someone listens to my thoughts, they might think I am crazy. I don't know what people think and I don't even care about others' thoughts. I am more of an introvert.

Only people close to me know how much of an extrovert I can be like my parents and Rose. Jane still isn't aware of me. Like Me. She might not even believe the reality of me being an extrovert.

I do enjoy my time here but there is something that keeps bothering me like what if these are my first and last days of enjoying the present. What if next year on this day I might be somewhere else?

No, stop.

I don't have the energy to think about something unnecessary as I have a bigger thing to focus on.

I was isolated for two days a few days back. I received a few parcels from mom while I was in the isolation ward. There are some entrepreneur classes for all. There we will be learning new entrepreneurial skills as it's common for both science and commerce.

Me and Jane met a girl a few days back and we were told that she will be joining us soon so we were very excited to shift to a new room which will completely belong to us.

We had an enrichment activity last week which was called 'the Ad Mad Show' and held in the assembly hall. It was a fun activity as it was like a competition between the four houses. We were given anonymous brands for which we were told to create an advertisement.

Each level had different emotions.

In the first level we were supposed to make an *emotional* advertisement. Next round was the *humour* round and it had two more rounds just like that. Me and Trevor are in the red house. Our house was disqualified in the first round itself because we could not complete the task better than the other houses. The winners of the show were green house. Jay and Jane were the leading members there.

Our class has established a company for the upcoming events and the company visits. We also recorded a video with our business studies teacher Mr. joe, introducing ourselves as the members of the team *UNIMOS*.

We are going to launch it officially soon in the assembly. After the company is launched and made official, we are going to organize our first event. Which will have my expertise in it as that is my favourite work to do.

Chapter 7

I was wrong. I thought making greeting cards would be fun as it is something I am interested in but I have been working on the cards for the past 5 days already.

It's fun to work together with the classmates as working together is making our bond much stronger and all of us are trying to get settled with each other slowly.

Me and Ethan did most of the work from cutting the sheets into a size of a card to folding them symmetrically. Trevor and Jane went to the city to purchase the necessary craft items. Cyrus was everywhere giving his help whenever needed.

Others were just wasting their time or we were giving them the work they could do without creating a mess like drawing pencil lines for me to write and then erasing them after I'm done.

Me and Jane were informed that our beds were shifted to another room as a new girl is supposed to join us soon. We were very excited to have a room to ourselves as we were previously sharing the room with Blair and Raquel.

It's not like they are bad company but it still feels good to have a room which I can call 'my room'.

After I was done shifting my wardrobe and other stuff completely, I was helping Jane shift hers. It is noon and we skipped sports to shift our stuff. I am standing beside Jane helping her pass the suitcase and she is standing on a chair and keeping her suitcases on the marble shelf above her wardrobe.

I chose the last compartment that is the 4th one. It has the best view. One window on right side of the bed and one in front. This room has a forest view from the back wall, yellow curtains, and yellow walls. Better than the pinkie one.

Thud.

Something fell.

Pieces on the floor.

The marble.

Blood!

Oh shit!

Blood is dripping from somewhere.

Someone is screaming.

Jane is falling from the chair and I give her support before she hits the floor hard. That's when I came to my senses and realised that the marble attached was loose.

The marble bar fell on Janes' nose and her head.

She is screaming like she just saw someone die in front of her and I remember she once told me that she is afraid of seeing blood even if it's her own.

Her eyes are shut tight but the blood is flowing from the top of her nose between the eyes.

I run towards my study table, grab a bunch of tissues without thinking and start to block her nose.

Now my hands are covered in jane's blood.

Jane is pushing me away as it might be hurting her a lot and I use force to block her hand movements to block the blood. She is still screaming but this time she is crying and saying her head hurts.

Repetitively.

I thought the marble fell on her head too and with a huge pressure but that's when I noticed that there is a long cut on her forehead where her hairline starts.

Oh Fish!

What should I do?

Giving her support with one hand for her to walk so that we could go to the doctor and covering her nose with my other hand, I try to make her stand. But, as soon as she stands, she falls.

Again.

Again.

And again.

That's when we made it out of the room somehow and hearing her screams some girls came running and I sent one of them to call our house parent. Our house parent along with Grace, Linda, Blair, and me carried her to the clinic.

The doctor says that she needs stitches and they take her to the city immediately. Fortunately, it was Saturday and some girls were there in the dorm.

Usually, some people skip sports on Saturdays. After Jane was gone, I cleaned the blood from our floor but it wasn't much to clean as I was right in time to use the tissues.

I threw away all the used tissues which were lying on the floor damp with blood. After the cleaning was done, I went for dinner and found out that Jane got 8 stitches on her nose and that she went home.

Something like this also happened a few days back. There was a girl from downstairs and all her friends were playing 'darkroom.' She was the seeker. She pushed the door of her room so forcefully that the glass attached to it came out and shattered on the floor.

She got 12 stitches on the head, 8 on neck and 15 on her palm. The corridor of the ground floor was covered in pool of blood as she walked on her own to the clinic. The incident happened in the middle of night and half of her friends started crying as they had insisted she play.

After Jane was gone, the room was evoking some weird feeling in me so I slept in with Grace, Linda, and Sarah in their room after we celebrated Sarahs' birthday eve.

*****

Ethan is now buttering me because he wants me to paint all 180 cards by myself. Not even in my dreams I am going to agree to that. We are in the class, facing each other. I am sitting in front of him to my assigned seat but I turned backwards. Mateo is sitting on his left and Trevor on his right.

"I'll do half of it and you guys take the other half" I counter.

"Come on... you have the potential to do all the work by yourself, I trust you can do it and I know you are willing to do it." Ethan says never stopping.

"How am I supposed to complete all of it by tomorrow and alone? You know that Jane is not supposed to come soon" My expressions showing just the opposite of what I said.

"You can do it alone; you have it in you. I know it. We all know it." His expression clearly showing he can never mean what he just said.

"Listen, whatever you need just tell me. I will bring you everything. Just do the painting part and give the rest of the things to the jerks wasting time." Ethan is now looking mischievously serious and the way he just told me everything now I think he really means what he said.

He won and I ended up taking all the burden on me.

Right now, I am sticking the cards on my room floor so that I can paint all of them at once. As I am going to be alone for the rest of the night in this room, I can fill the floor completely.

I stuck 45-50 cards at once and waited for them to dry after I was done with painting them. I somehow managed to complete my work within 3 hours. Then I remembered that I gave 40 cards to Ethan so that the guys could show some creativity.

I came to class the other morning and I saw all the cards which they prepared kept on my table, they really did some good work. "I'm impressed" that's what I wanted to say when Ethan and Cyrus were walking to the classroom carrying more stuff.

"You could have done better, I alone did more and better work as compared to you people" I was not even aware of the thought but this is what left my mouth.

"Then you should have done it yourself" Ethan hissed.

Did I just piss Ethan off?

Was he already pissed at something and my comment made it much worse? Cyrus is eyeing me to shut my mouth whereas I am being completely brainless.

"I am not working on this scrap." I make a disgusting look.

The look on Cyruss' face is telling me I have said something I shouldn't have. Ethan throws the box he was carrying on the table and he is leaving the class just when Trevor arrives.

"Impressed?" Trevor asks me, and Ethans' back facing me, Cyrus is staring me. All three of them waiting for the response.

"Well... it's neither bad nor perfect. It's simple and...... good"

Ethan stomped out of the class and Cyrus was shaking his head like he was going crazy. Trevor released a sigh of relief.

"What's up with him?" I ask both pointing at the crazy going Ethan just when Mateo arrives.

Trevor is now facing Mateo

"Will you care to give an explanation?" Mateo nods. Now facing me.

"All of us slept after having some fun and we completely forgot about the cards. Ethan did most of the work alone as he had no other choice. Jay, Cyrus, and Trevor woke up in the middle of night and helped him with the finishing" He finishes.

So that's the reason why he is pissed. I was not the reason for it but my comment added fuel to the fire.

"Did you say anything?" Mateos' question to me, made Cyrus jump in between to answer even when no one asked him.

"She literally got herself killed. He would have killed her already if she would have said anything other than *useless* stuff" his hands on his head.

"I never used the word useless" I shrug.

"It sounded like you mean it" He is grabbing his hair out of frustration.

"Sounding like it and meaning it are two different things" I corrected him. Of course they are different.

"You both are hurting my ears. Just leave the class and kill each other outside" we both jump on Ethans' voice.

He is staring at both me and Cyrus like he is going to eat us alive if we don't stop.

"He has a loose screw." I curse under my breath so that everyone standing close to me can listen except Ethan when I leave the class.

Chapter 8

Jane was back after two days. I did a really good job the past few days which was trying my best not to murder one of my annoying classmates.

Working with crazy Ethan on the last moment for bookmarks, watching Jane and Trevor getting along well whereas Cyrus was taking all the credit for the cards I made by spreading false rumours that he did all the work. Others were helping to sort the cards according to the price list.

The day is finally here. Today is the day of our sale. Every weekend we had an enrichment activity. Movies are fixed but sometimes for new learning and sometimes for refreshment. The stupids' of science- I mean the students of science were told to organize a fun maths activity in the auditorium after lunch.

I was busy organizing the tables for the sale with Ethan, Trevor, and Jane. All of us reached late for the program and ended up leaving early.

Thanks to Mr. Aden, we were saved from that mathematics trauma. It was crazy how they were using equations to create any shape and the craziest part was to watch the maths teacher draw different figures. He drew a legit dinosaur using some big freaking equation.

The kids were creating a huge fuss for the sale so I started shouting randomly at them. They were pushing the tables, pulling each other, some even started fighting for the same card they found attractive. In short, our sale was a great success.

None of us thought that we would be short of stock. Some kids left disappointed as they did not reach on time and went back empty handed.

Some were still hoping that I could make a new card for them. I felt bad for them as even if I wanted to make a few cards I couldn't do it because I am out of resources.

There was a prevailing sense of immense relief after the sale. I was pleased that every drop of sweat was worth it in the end. The commerce department was jumping with joy and the exhaustion was easily visible on everyone's face.

After we cleaned up our area there were some tags remaining. Those tags had price and the category like 'for boys, for girls' written on it as it was for differentiating the counter.

Everyone started sticking those tags on each other's bags and were taunting each other for the same. It was funny to see high schoolers do something so childish. I started leaving and they all followed me. Suddenly I could *hear* silence.

What happened to them? I wanted to turn around and look at what they were up to but I could feel their footsteps behind me. I turned around to look at their faces and everyone stopped.

Then they started laughing. Jane eyed me to look at my bag and.... All the stickers were now on my bag and some were even stapled. I ran to grab Cyrus as I knew it was his idea but all of them helped him escape. It was a hilarious moment though.

We all really need some proper sleep. I really need a proper sleep.

*****

After we were done with the calculation, we found that we really did a great job and made an amazing profit. It was

Sunday again. It was some sort of belief our class followed. It was the only thing we all had in common which was.

No.

Breakfast.

On.

Sundays.

Four words, simple meaning.

I. Need. More. Sleep.

This was the untold rule of our class. Though there are some stupid's who give the first preference to food rather than sleep. I would kill if someone woke me for some damn food from my fantasy. Same boring Sunday it was. Pass just the same.

Speaking of fantasy, I remembered that I still have the most interesting part left to read from the novel I was reading. I was just starting to read when the door of my room opened.

Sarah entered carrying a bucket, Blair has a water bottle, Grace is standing with her tuck box, and Linda is holding a wooden box in her hand.

What the...?

They are sitting in random places in my room and.... Wait what?

"Don't tell me that you guys are planning for an orchestra" In my room. Without me knowing.

"Go and get your instruments" Sarah orders.

And now I have two scales and Jane is using two spoons. We started with slow songs and after three hours we were screaming to hard rock.

Some of our juniors have already requested us to keep our voices low but we won't listen. We gave ourselves a break during lunch time. Then all of us again started with our orchestra. We were warned by the security guard and our house parent almost six times as it was midnight already. For others.

We finally stopped when none of us had the strength to speak. It was a great time and a new great memory was added to my collection. Now finally everyone disappeared in their rooms. Jane was fast asleep. I was giving a final touch to my packing.

*****

I'm waiting desperately for my parents to arrive at the admin block. The bus is dropping a bunch of parents at a time. Jane said 'I think I saw your father' I jumped and started running behind the bus.

That's when I noticed that a bunch of people were running behind me and shouting 'slow down!! You'll fall, don't run!' I ignored all the voices like they were talking to someone else.

When I saw my father standing in front of the dining hall, I just jumped on him and started crying.

Chapter 9

That day was very awesome as I spent it with my family. They welcomed me at home with a 'welcome home' cake and congratulations-on-passing-a-month-in-almost-jail banner. Like I am really coming back from prison. Balloons all over my room.

I came back to school after a ten-day break. While coming back we went to Janes' house and stayed there a bit then we headed to school together. once we were finally inside, we heard rumours that a new guy joined the science stream in our class.

It's been a week and everything is normal on schedule. Except for one thing. The new guy who was famous for his looks. He is nothing much then a piece of trash to me. People were saying he looks like our senior. Few were saying our senior is doing 11th again and most of the people were saying they are twins, that's bullshit. He doesn't even look like him a bit and he is good for nothing. I found him a lot more annoying than one could have imagined.

The school is going to celebrate the thanksgiving festival celebrated by farmers, to acknowledge the importance of bulls and oxen.

We are taken to a big ground somewhere outside the campus. Now that the program has started, I'm getting bored.

"Why is the weather so hot?" I'm annoyed by the voice and I don't have to look to identify the speaker. Wait… what was his name? I never bothered to know as the sound of his voice irritates me.

Before I could think of a savage reply we both were looking at the speaker who interrupted the one-sided conversation,

"Goddammit Bryan, What's wrong with you?" Ignoring the atmosphere Henry continuous to speak

"You are sitting right in front of the air cooler."

Before me being dragged in this I replied, "get lost you both, go and fight somewhere else" and ignoring my irritating tone goddammit Bryan continues to throw unnecessary words out of his fool mouth

"Want some juice?" he points the fresh juice at me.

Does this jerk have a death wish? Can't he see me ignoring him all along or is he so blind that he can't even see my bottle of juice in my hand?

"Can't you see that I already have my own?" I say already annoyed.

"I was just asking because I don't like this flavour" he says acting innocent. His one hand point to the juice in the other hand.

"Just keep it away then" I scoff getting harsh now.

"Chill bro, I was just being nice" he smirks.

Eww.

Oh, you don't have to, I don't even care about you being nice. I stomped out of that area and found another place to sit. Me and Jane are now enjoying the program with our juniors. The weather is hot and my favourite purple shirt is soaked in sweat.

There is a lady sitting next to me and I asked her if she could give me her phone so that I can call my mom and let her know that I wish to come back home.

After crying on the call with my mom I felt relieved.

Most of the students here were so homesick that they would cry all the time. I am not one of them but I thought if I don't go for a break I might get influenced.

We had our lunch there itself. The food was served on a banana leaf and the sitting arrangement was organized under a huge shade.

We are taken back to school before evening.

Now that we are back, I am deciding whether to go for sports or not. I feel lazy to go for sports just after coming back. I also must wash my clothes first and a bath is necessary.

The laziness won.

It's been an hour since I made a study plan so that I am not left behind in academics and it is lying on my bed unfinished, I am reading a novel.

I was so lost in the novel that I didn't notice that Jane was back early from the sports. I just remembered that I had a scheduled call with my parents today at sports time.

As there are not electronics allowed, the students had seven calls allowed per year. They could use it anytime they want but before using it you must submit the call slip a day before taking the call.

I came back from the call and begged my parents to take me home as I am feeling sick. My parents promised me they'll come to get me next week but, before that there is a real challenge coming up.

EXAMS.

The next day of the festival of bulls and oxen there was a general knowledge quiz competition among the houses and the red house came first from the bottom of the leader board, credit goes to Trevor.

Chapter 10

It's been a few days since the new girl joined. On her first day we got *really* close. We got to know each other's history, politics, and geography.

I regret it now. I'm not that type of person who likes to talk behind peoples backs still, you never know all about others. I mean I just met her that day and over-shared everything.

Speaking of her, I've been isolated since Kinsey came. Same class as me and Jane. I have not been well for the past three days and I'll be discharged in the next two days.

The thing that upsets me the most is that Jane and Kinsey haven't visited me once till now. I don't expect anything from people but sometimes it feels like why do I care *extra* for them.

Whenever Jane used to get isolated, I visited her more than 4 times a day. It doesn't feel good when you do something for someone and they just take it for granted.

I believe they are busy studying hard but, they could spare a minute for me at least.

Whatever, I shouldn't care.

The strangest thing is that for the sake of being a classmate Bryan asked me how I am feeling, he is the only person who made some effort to ask me whenever we crossed paths during lunch or dinner. Well, I guess he's not that bad after all.

Moreover, exams are going on right now. I am giving my exams from the isolation ward itself.

I kept begging the doctor to call my mom but she kept refusing. The doctors are supposed to give calls to the students if they are in the isolation ward for more than three days but she won't let me talk.

I slept for nearly three hours after giving today's exam. When I was finally up after another session of being unconscious, I was surprised to see Jane holding a parcel for me. That was from my mom. She was acting like someone forced her to bring it to me.

She handed me the parcel and then she asked me how I was feeling. Nevertheless, she was acting a bit strange. I didn't ask her the reason because I know just like always, she would made some excuse. Also, Kinsey didn't come to see me.

She might have been busy.

I keep distracting myself from the thought of being alone.

I am discharged the next day and I went to the principal's office to check whether he would permit me to go home or not. unfortunately, the principal didn't allow me to go home as he said they have some protocols.

My parents will surely get me out somehow.

Upcoming Monday is teachers' day and the seniors are called for the decoration to the assembly hall on Sunday.

Again, Sundays are only for sleep. No work. It is a rule to enjoy sleep on Sunday. Not only for me but for more than half of the population in the school. I woke up lazily and finally got ready in a whole hour.

I never expected today to be so amazing and full of fun. I am sitting on the floor with my seniors. They are helping me with the card cutting, Blair and Sarah are helping me with the paint and Trevor and Ethan are rubbing salt on an open wound.

Not exactly wound but when someone asked who prepared the cards on companies launch, Ethan and Trevor kept shouting my name.

Ethan prepared the list for the students who will be helping in the decoration and he forgot to add Kinsey's name. Ethan only added a few names and hence All wanted to have fun, all the boys went on the stage and started dancing like Mateo as he is not here.

Jay got a cut on his right thumb as he was trying to impress everyone around him by cutting the hard board sheet with a sharp cutter in one go. He swung his hand in the air and said "Oh shoot… that's not big enough"

While saying that, his blood droplets scattered around everywhere. Two on my pj's, one on the incomplete card, three in front of Ethans' foot and a few on himself.

What a mess.

Me and Ethan grabbed him and dragged him all the way towards the water cooler behind the assembly hall to wash of the evidence.

We had the music system to ourselves and we completed the work while listening to songs, enjoying ourselves. All of us skipped Sports as it is a lot of work to do. The work was finally done before dinner time and all of us went for dinner.

Exhausted.

*****

Today's Teachers Day, and I am really confused.

How is it celebrated here? The program took place in the assembly itself. All of us felicitated all the teachers one by one. It was fun, we went for classes but this time not for studying rather for teaching.

Except for the seniors we are allotted positions in the junior classes. I was given class 5th and 6th grade which is the lowest grade here. It is fun playing with the kids, we played a lot of games together. We also had an interview session and I got to know more about them and they got to know more about me.

While I am in Class 5, A cranky classmate of mine came and started talking about bikes. these kids are nearly 10, like what is wrong with this guy?

He doesn't know how to talk and what to talk about at what place. I left the class as fast as I could and I am relieved.

I called everyone out of their classes after lunch as we had a movie schedule. The teachers decided the movie, it's a thriller and very boring. I never thought I would be watching a movie like this in my life. Some of the students were half asleep and some completely slept off.

Today's day was very exhausting and playful too. It is Jane's birthday tomorrow and I am very excited for it. It is a ritual to decorate the compartment of the birthday girl and I decided to do so. Me and Kinsey started with the decoration and pasted a note on the main door of our room which said "No Jane allowed."

"Did you hear something?" I asked Kinsey while she was blowing balloons.

"Nope, what is it?" she looked at me in confusion.

"Nothing... I think I heard someo-"

Thud.

Before I could complete my sentence, I heard something. Like someone hit a rock on our window.

Thud.

This time Kinsey heard it too.

"Boohoo!!!!!!"

We jumped.

Turned on the bigger light.

Something is near the window.

Someone is there.

I remove the curtains completely to get a better look on the person other side.

"Oh shi- are you crazy!!! Get the hell out of here!" I screamed.

Jane was standing in the window all along.

I was so stunned I would have thrown something at her if it wasn't her birthday. She left laughing through the corridor and vanished in Sarah's room. We continued to decorate her compartment.

We did our best, sticky notes with motivational and self-boosting quotes all over her study table, I wrote some funny tag-lines we use for her on the balloons, we also attached a 'Happy birthday' banner above her bed. That was all we could do with the limited resources and time.

It is finally time to call her in the room. She came excited and she is astonished. Her expression is the only thing needed for us to tell that she really liked it all. We are satisfied that the time we spent was worth it.

Chapter 11

Today is fun.

At Least for me.

I prepared a treasure hunt for Jane a.k.a. the 'birthday girl'. I gave some sort of hints to some of our classmates. The person with the hint had a dare for her and if she completes it, she gets the hint from that person to the other.

I had the first clue which said "monkey-like face, Mr. attitude" she guessed it correctly in the first guess. I am the only one who skipped the dare part. Ethan gave her a dare and the clue he had followed to the other person.

The day has come to an end. She still hasn't found her treasure and I don't even know where she is. All the walls in the art class are filled with paintings made by students till now.

There are three long benches, each kept in front of three walls. I am sitting on the last one with Ethan and Mr. Pedrot. I can see Kinsey helping Cyrus and they are sitting exactly opposite to us. The bench on my right is filled with other idiots of my class and the area on my left, the front of fourth wall is filled with the ceramic articles brought here as panting references for art students.

Mr. Pedrot is giving everyone a canvas with a reference image to paint something of our choice.

I am searching for something to paint but my eye caught upon Ethan's mess. He is destroying his canvas and he knows it too.

"Give it to me, I can't bear to see the beautiful canvas turning into a piece of trash." I spoke. Expressionless.

He just laughed at himself and handed it to me quietly. The Ethan I knew would just glare at me, is always full of himself and would never take someone's help OR help someone.

"Are you taking up my offer of help?" I ask surprised.

"Oh no, you got me wrong, I'm not taking your help. I'm letting you do the work for me that you wanted to do by yourself." He smiles, hands crossed over his chest.

"How can someone be this shameless? At Least thank me I'm saving the canvas and paints from you"

At least.

"You're welcome, what paints do you need other than these, any tool required?" He smirked.

He can be a total prick sometimes. While I am doing my work ~~his work~~ peacefully, he wanted to show me something in the painting and he took it from me. Just in that time trouble found us.

His second name is trouble.

He poured some drops of dirty water which was kept for cleaning the brush on Ethans' painting.

"You bloody little pi–" before I could complete my sentence Ethan grabbed him by his collar. Ethan started shouting like hell.

"What the hell is wrong with you, you bastard, you piece of shi–" Ethan blasts.

"Chill man it's just water, you can fix–" he tries to speak

oh, come on why does he want everyone to chill? Now I am getting very irritated.

"What chill? Who the hell are you to tell me what to do, do you even have something up there or it's completely empty like I have known?" Ethan shoved him aside just when Mr. Pedrot came shouting for him to leave Bryan.

There is always some new drama in the art class and especially when the teacher leaves for a second. I hoped Ethan would have slapped that jerk. He ruined my hard work.

"You could have slapped him; it would have felt a lot better" I said gritting my teethes.

"I was about to" he said in a very disappointing tone.

Don't know why but, I felt relieved that I'm not the only person who feels irritated by him. Speaking of that, it always looks like Ethan and Bryan are not on good terms.

Now that the atmosphere is little cooled, I spot Jane standing in the doorway.

I can tell by her face she is not at all feeling well. She always wanted her birthday to be a big deal. Maybe that's why her mood is spoiled.

I called her and asked what happened and just like always she refused to tell me. As I could see there was no point in continuing the game, I asked Trevor to give her the gift as he was the last person in the clue Cyrus had.

The gift is nothing more than a greeting card all of us made together for her. I am not sure if she liked it or not as her mood is completely different as compared to the morning.

She walks to the door and calls Mr. Pedrot outside and says something, he tells her to leave. She didn't even look at me once.

Maybe she is going to get some rest.

Now that she is gone, I see the scary senior stomping off to his class. I have noticed that he and Jane got close as he treated her like his younger sister. They both always go for sports together. Also, he is not scary. I just thought that because of his beard and the hairs covering his eyes.

Rufus is like an elder brother. Cyrus told me that Jane and Rufus had a fight, that is the reason for her bad mood.

Whatever, they have argued a lot before too. I went to the dormitory after the class and found Jane packing her stuff.

Loading......

Processing......

Uploaded......

She.

Is.

Leaving.

"How?" without wasting time on asking questions like when and why she was going I asked her how she got the permission.

"Well... I had a long talk with the principal. I couldn't breathe here. I don't feel good. I'm grateful for whatever you did for me and I really appreciate it. I'll be back next week." She replied weakly and grabbed her suitcase.

"I hope you recover well at home, have a good time." I said holding her hand.

We hugged and I felt relieved for her. She was looking disturbed for the past few weeks. Kinsey went for sports an hour ago and I'm alone. I already have a lot on my plate and I need a bit of rest for now so guess I should just sleep.

Rage

We scream, we shout, we cry out loud
We throw, we punish, we break down
We fear, we believe, we resist
The thought, the action, the emotion
It reacts, it repels, it reminds of the reality
The truth, the idea, the feeling
Forces the spontaneity to response
Just like a cat hunting its prey
Just like fire catching the fuel
We seek the opportunity to pour out our energy
We might think we have caught the track
But rage will drag us down the path

Chapter 12

"You sure you'll be fine?" I am not sure how Kinsey is going to live alone as Jane is also not here.

"Just get well soon and come back soon, I really want you to return soon. Till then Jane will be back so don't worry" Kinsey assured.

"*That's* the only thing I'm worried about. ha-ha…" I replied. Jane and Kinsey never got along well. I am the only means for them to talk with each other.

I got to know that my parents are coming for me because of my health conditions. The school has permitted a leave for 3 days. Jane went the day before yesterday and I'll be back the day after tomorrow's day.

This *was* the plan.

Unfortunately, I got typhoid when I was home. Also, I had to extend my 3 days leave to a week. After coming back, I noticed things have changed. A lot.

Between Jane and me.

WHY? What is it? Jane has been avoiding me since I came back and even after living in the same room, we just greet each other once a day and it's hard to look each other in the eyes.

"What is wrong with you?" We are in our room and I finally asked her as it is impossible to avoid the awkward air.

"Shouldn't I be the one to ask you this?" she hissed.

"What? You are the on-" before I could complete, she snapped back.

"Kinsey told me everything, I'm not a fool. Quit acting now, you are not what you look like" she said with tears in her eyes.

what is wro-

OH, I regretted the night I over-shared everything with Kinsey.

Jane and I both found each other a little irritating sometimes and don't know what mad dog bit me. I shared a little part of my feelings about Jane, with Kinsey.

It was not only me sharing with her but she also said about how Jane used to talk behind my back whenever I wasn't around and that's why I *trusted* her.

"What about you huh? Tell me you never said anything about me. When I was ill didn't you said I am acting just to get some attention." I snapped back.

Now we are talking.

I am glaring at Kinsey.

She is mouthing to me that she is sorry.

We all are sitting on my bed. Me and Jane facing each other whereas Kinsey is hiding behind Jane. As Jane could not see her, she is acting like she didn't have a choice and she regretted what she did. The session went on for another hour and finally the conclusion is that we stopped talking, Jane went to the restroom and Kinsey finally spoke.

"I'm sor-" she tried to speak only to get cut off in mid-sentence.

"Stop. Just stop. I don't want to listen to your bullshit." I got up and stood in front of my wardrobe.

I am getting angry.

What was this?

Lack of trust?

False hope?

Betrayal?

Rage?

Yes.

"Trust me, just once" she spoke again.

"BULLSHIT! Trust you? Do you even know the meaning of trust? Do you even know how it feels once it's broken? Oh right, how would you know? you are one of the people breaking it. A wise lady once said; 'Trust is like a glass, once broken. It'll never be the same' I don't have the energy to deal with the mess you have created right now." I stopped. My heart pounding and tears held in my eyes.

Enough for the night I thought but, I added "*Trust me*, you are a bitch and *you know it*." I switched off the lights and climbed my bed.

No good nights, no good mornings, no hellos,' no byes. The three of us didn't talk for the next three days.

Jane got sick, I took her to the doctor and she discussed our argument with the doctor. The doctor suggested we talk once more. we sorted things out on our own and finally the conclusion was that Kinsey exaggerated and provoked both of us.

Jane and Ethan went to the city for some check-ups, it's been a week since that argument and both of us are trying our best to avoid Kinsey most of the time.

Jane and Ethan came back during Lunch time and as we demanded our economics teacher to give us some free time, he agreed and told us to do whatever we liked. All of us sat in front of our class and occupied our usual spots.

Ethan started with singing the songs from our assembly. He and Trevor are sitting exactly opposite to me in the porch. Then we made funny versions of each and every song.

After a while Jane suggested playing a game of "pole to pole". Each player must keep touching a pole. If any player leaves the pole and the chaser touches it, it's his/hers'.

Everyone must keep switching the poles with his/her fellow mates and it's fun to make plans to switch with someone and trick them and switch with someone else so that a person is stuck.

This continues till you are barely standing or in simple words, tired. The porch in between our two classes of commerce and science has a lot of poles. It's the best spot to play this.

Ethan planned to switch with Trevor. Then asked me to switch with him. I was unaware of the devil's plan so I agreed.

Ethan asked me to switch with him and just when I left my pole, he grabbed it but instead of Trevor grabbing Ethan's pole, Henry jumped and took that pole. I ran and grabbed Henry's pole.

Now this is fun.

Trevor ended up being stuck as his pole was already taken by Mateo who was chasing us from the past 15 minutes. This all happened so fast that other than us no-one could understand what exactly happened. After that I stopped trusting Ethan and I started calling him a cheater.

The science people came back from the physics lab and they were staring at us in confusion like what the hell happened that made all of us laugh so hard. The people crossing our class were also staring at us surprised.

This is the first time all of us played something together. Especially outside the class. One of the most memorable moments I created with my classmates.

More to come.

Chapter 13

English classes were the best. Our English teacher is very knowledgeable and he knows exactly what's going on in someone's mind. I always wait for the English class as there are always new words waiting for me.

Mr. Brandon uses new words in every class to communicate with us to increase our vocabulary. In today's class all of us requested him to play pole-to-pole as it is a new fun activity discovered by us.

All of us played like kids, even Mr. Brandon is surprised after watching us getting along well.

I gave Ethan a letter for my mom as he is going home due to his illness.

Yesterday there was a seminar outside the campus. There we had tea and biscuits for the first time in a while. The snack arrangement was made in an open lawn. A table for tea and biscuits was kept in a corner. That was the first time I drank tea on my will AND didn't hate it. I am *not* a tea person.

*****

Its Wednesday again, Wednesday means fun day. Yesterday I had fever in afternoon and it's the same today. My voice is gone and throat feels like someone stuffed a cactus in it. The doctor asked me to get admitted in the isolation ward but I really want to attend today's art class. Me and Jay stated to fight with paint and Kinsey is helping Cyrus. A lot of fun and a ton of scolding form the doctor for being late. When I am in my room, my house parent suddenly burst into the room "you girls don't understand anything! I have been telling you to be there during breakfast on time but you all won't listen! Now the principal wants all of you in his cabin. Now!" she is shouting like the earth is flat because of us.

Kinsey has gone for sports and I am packing my essentials for the isolating ward. Jane and I follow our house parent to the principal's office. We explain our reason for being late, which is nothing but our PT teacher leaving us late from the morning PT and it takes time to shower. Hygiene is a must. He scolds us a little and then we are free.

Once I'm in the isolation ward, I talk to my mom.

I leave for dinner.

During dinner Bryan passed me a book

"Make sure you open it alone." He whispered while crossing me.

I opened it when I am all alone in the isolation ward, a letter.

It is addressed to me.

Off-course it is.

I open it.

Read it.

It explains everything.

How Jane and Rufus got into a fight. Every detail of what happened that day in art class while I was busy dealing with Ethan.

The writing itself was enough for me to know the sender of this piece of paper.

Next day, I am having lunch in the dining hall with no one beside me. Alone. I pick a bite to shove it in my mouth and when it's almost close to my lips, suddenly a voice whisper

"When are you returning my book?"

I could feel the air of his spoken words on my ear.

I jump sideways and see a long figure standing behind me carrying the same irritating smile on his face. I shout.

"What the HELL is wrong with you BRYAN!!??" I could have just thrown the plate on his face if it wasn't one of the few things I eat without complaining.

"Tell Rufus the reply will take some time" I spoke again. Normally this time.

That guy basically told me to believe his side of the story and not Janes', she is also a good friend of mine, I must give it some thought.

Bryan is still standing on my head. Oh, the book.

"Is it fine if I return it tonight? On the other hand, why are you even reading about history?" I mean this stuff is for people with some brains. I keep this part to myself.

"Ahh! It fascinates me" the smile never leaving his face.

I never thought this guy could read.

Days turned into a week and I was discharged. However, there is an event held in the market in heart of the city for which our school is taken early morning. Fortunately, due to my weakness I am not allowed to go.

Someone wakes me up.

"What?" I growl barely opening my eyes. But when I tried, there are wide open because of another 5 pair of eyes staring back at me.

"Do you have white pants?" Raquel asks

"Pair of hair clips?" Blair joins her

"And a white stole" Jane finishes.

"What time is it?" this is the only thing I care about right now.

"Its 4:30...... A.M." Grace replies. I go blank. What the hell are they even doing in my room demanding my stuff?

Loading...

Processing...

finding upcoming events... Ahh event!

Uploading...

THAT event!

I give them whatever they needed. I sleep.

My alarm ~~beeps~~ blasts. Eyes wide open, again. Wild hair, creased clothes, dizzy head. I grab my tooth brush and stroll towards the bathroom.

As soon as I step out of my room, I feel nice. The silence echoing in hostel feels like a soothing music to my body from head to toe.

No unnecessary screaming and shouting girls, no time bound for classes.

Once I am back after doing my stuff, I stand in front of my wardrobe searching for the cloths I planned to wear out with my mom.

Yesterday, doctor told me that my mom was going to come for me as I am in a very bad shape. Also, due to this I didn't go for the event. I am supposed to visit the clinic in an hour to get an update about my mom's arrival.

I grab the black T-shirt hanging on my chair and put it on. I untangle my bed hair just when door to my room abruptly opened.

I ~~knew~~ thought I was alone.

Chapter 14

The sun is bright outside. The driver stops in front of the nearest hotel. We go in, call my dad and my brother.

It's been 2 hours since my mom busted in my room, I was so shocked at that time that I forgot what organs are used for moving. She ran towards me and hugged me tightly.

Unfortunately, things didn't go as planned. As soon as we reach the main gate, all the buses arrived in the campus. We planned to leave and be back before the students but, they arrived before we could leave. Jane rushed towards our car and started crying for how did the school allowed my mom to take me.

Leaving everyone behind, we directly went to the nearest medical to get intravenous drip. Sooner after that we reached the hotel, had breakfast and it was time for mom to leave me in the campus again. It was the first time in 2 years of me getting an IV drip.

It felt nice.

The doctor tried to insert the pin in my hands 3 times but failed. She called her husband who is more practiced than her, he was successful in first attempt.

Jane fed me dinner. Sat with me for some time and once the IV drip is finished, I am discharged.

Again.

*****

Dear Dairy,

Days passed; it was time for another assembly for me to conduct. GH-3 (girls' hostel-3) first floor performed an assembly and our theme was traditional culture. Everyone was dressed in some traditional cloths and performed a dance. Except me.

I gave vote of thanks. I am more into speaking than dancing or singing. The following day we had a dance night. It's a tradition and our school follow it. I participated in that because everyone was too busy to judge anyone.

Juniors to seniors, everyone was busting in our room just for getting a perfect eyeliner touch from Kinsey. Rushing here and there, both of us got all dressed up at last.

She was wearing a greyish skirt-top cord set. Her curly black hair bouncing on her shoulders as she moved. Jane was in black square neck top with the traditional red skirt whereas I wore a high neck jet-black crop top with embroidery on both of its shoulders with a peacock green floor touching skirt.

Exams have started but I feel like I am not well prepared. I must work hard.

Well don't have much so that's it for now.

OH WAIT!

I remember an incident from a few days back.

It was 2 A.M. everyone in the hostel was sleeping, including Kinsey. I somehow felt Jane was awake. I was looking out of the window in the dark forest and suddenly a light passed my eyes.

I got attentive to see where did the light came from.

"I thing I saw someone using a flashlight on my window" I whispered.

I could hear Jane sitting up and opening her window a little. It was a dark night. No lights in the room. Only the sound of insects and the ceiling fan.

A thud.

Someone screamed.

I screamed.

I have no idea why but I did.

I turned around Kinsey was gone.

She was not in her bed.

Janes' bed was behind mine but due to the outfit changing compartment between our beds, there was no visibility for us to see each other whereas Kinseys' bed was opposite to Janes', she was in a cross from me in the other half of the room. Her part was visible to both of us.

"What was THAT?!" I shouted.

"You crazy idiot! Who stands like this?!" Jane said. But not to me.

Turns out, Kinsey was curious about the light outside and she didn't realise her hair were all over her face. She stood quietly behind Jane and when Jane turned, she saw Kinsey's horrifying face from close. Her green eyes shining from the little lamp outside.

They both screamed together and what I did was a reflex, scream for scream.

This was one of the terrifyingly funniest time we had.

Done with today's dairy update. I haven't been writing a lot but this is for my parents to know my mundane life. For me to never forget some bits and pieces of my life. My father's birthday is coming up soon and terms starting from the next day.

I have requested to a call although its will be Sunday that day and the offices will be closed.

Fortunately, I got the permission.

*****

This morning when I reached the class, I saw someone standing in front of the door wearing a cap in mid-monsoon season. I went closer to get a better look on the persons face.

"Hey! Sup!? Why are you wearing a cap?" I asked Jay.

He replied "I was cutting my hair last night. Ethan offered to help. Don't laugh" He didn't elaborate further and removed his cap.

I gasped.

A big funny smile got to my face. I couldn't help but laugh at the shiny bald head of his.

"Ethan messed up the back of my head and it would have been a lot weirder if I had kept the remaining hair looking like a pineapple" He turned away as he tried not to show the embarrassment on his face.

I feel bad for him from the bottom of my heart. I could be lying if I said this.

Its been two hours since the classes started.

All of us are sleeping with our eyes wide open. We have our business exam tomorrow and everyone looks like for the first time we have studied more than enough.

"Get up, come on let's go."

It's been 10 minutes since Mr. Joe dragged us out the class to the meditation point which is at the top of 250 stairs. As we climbed up to the nature's beauty, we did a quick revision and Mr. Joe made us play some games. Nice group of people. Fun activity. Cold breeze. Dosen of photos. Nice calming view of the city.

"Aur kya chaiye?" *what more do you want?*

We played a couple of games and I got a pen as a reward for winning one of those games. we walked for a mile and realised we had to go back to the class. We headed straight towards the class for another sleepy session as due to terms, no teacher was teaching anything new and the classes were just for self-preparation.

I didn't realise this is going to be my last "IN-school interaction" with Jane. She said a few times that she won't be joining in the next term and she did sound serious.

Chapter 15

10 Days Later

SHIT.

Chapter 16

Mr. Aden is REALLY pissed at me.

The holidays we got after term exams were for a week. Not an extra day. I re-joined after 10 days and the first person I saw in the campus was none other than Mr. Aden. I got a good amount of scolding from him.

It took me at least 4 hours to unpack my luggage.

Next day, I am submitting my projects to all the teachers when Ethan notices my project cover page in commerce class.

"Hey Olivi, make one for me" this is an order rather than a request. He points his index finger at my project.

"What will I get in return?" if this is a give and take deal, I'm in.

"Oh... in return.... I'll give you almonds" He smiles.

Wha- is he for real? Does he really think I'll waste my creativity for some *almonds*?

"Are you crazy? This project contains marks. I need something more even though this is just a page." I say holding my hair up as due to the humid weather I am soaking in sweat.

He faces Mateo and whispers something to him. Now he is facing me again with a little devilish smile on his face. He is up to something for sure.

"Here is the offer, I'll give you my snacks for today and you will make me cover pages for all the subjects." His arms crossed over his chest.

He really is a chicken head.

"Are you seriou-" and before I could say anything he goes on

"If you don't like this offer, I have many more. Like, Mateo will give you his wafers, or I will give you almonds plus peanuts. And if this doesn't work, keep my one pack of fryums. One more thing, keep my chocolate. Not with the fryums of course. Now you must agree, I have never traded my chocolate. Ever." He is standing in front of me. Hands in his pockets and smiling like a monkey.

I do agree with the fact that I have never seen him giving his chocolate to anyone. Though I have seen him taking chocolates from the kids.

"I will think about it." I will make him beg me more. But I will make it for him in the end.

"The offer(s) won't be there forever" he has a playful tone. This makes me want to steal all the stuff he offered right now.

All of us headed towards the auditorium for the dance practice.

The theme for this years' founders' day is independence. Every class is given some dance steps to practice and so is ours. Once done with the fight, everyone started the practice. Excluding me. Like I said, I not a dance person.

However, I will be the host this year on founders' day throughout the event. I am glad to have this opportunity and I won't let anyone take it away. Although I do not have my script now, me and Bryan are given the task to keep the progress update of all the classes as we are short on days.

Some of my fellow mates are tired and came to rest. I asked Ethan again what he is going to give me. I got a response just like typical-crazy-Ethan would respond.

"I'll give you my friendship in exchange for the cover pages." *He looks at me as if he is offering me a nuclear bomb code.*

"Are we not friends?" I asked him in the same tone he talks to me.

Mischievous.

"Oh....... we... are... Friends? Hehe... I thought we were just classmates...." He scratches his head.

Now I must think of something to match his level.

"Ok. I don't need your friendship. I just need something useful. Which your friendship isn't. Obviously." I shrug.

"That hurts... I am giving you, MY friendship. You are hurting me. This is not expected from you." He shows clearly no signs of what he just said.

"Well now that I have made it clear that I don't need your friendship, what are you really going to give me?" I am more than satisfied by annoying him. The look on his face is worth it.

He kept convincing me and I agreed by the end of the day. It was fun making a deal in exchange for friendship like we are 10.

It took a few days to make all the cover pages and when I was making one in the class, Trevor saw me and he also demanded some. "Ugh, exhausting..."

*****

I'm scared.

So very scared that if a press any key on the keyboard, I'm doomed. Everything is on the display.

Every detail.

The founders' day script came in our native language and that is the problem. I don't know how to read half of the words and the scrip writer, who so ever it is, has a terrible hand writing. The script was sent to Mr. Scott online.

He took us to the staff room for re-typing the script. While he was explaining some part for the script to Jay and Bryan, I opened my mail and sent a few updates to my parents. This is not allowed. Contacting parents without a teachers' consent is not allowed.

It's illegal. I did it anyway.

After all, only a fool would miss this opportunity.

Howsoever, Mr. Scott faced me and started with the explanation. My mails are open. Moreover, my parents are replying. They are online.

Mr. Scott is so busy with the explanation that he won't notice my screen but, if I touch a single key, he will get distracted. I decided to remain still.

He got a call.

He got up.

He left.

God bless the person on the other side.

He came back. "let's continue tomorrow. You also leave."

We left.

Not yet. It is still 20 minutes left for dinner and my conversation with mom is not complete. Bryan handed me the original script prints and three of us ran towards the computer lab.

As I was already translating the script in English I had a valid reason to go, they both are already IT students. Whenever someone who is not an IT student enters the lab, the on-duty teacher asks for the reason to access the computers and a consent letter from the principal. No one would ask why did we go there.

I clicked on my moms' unread mail.

She is not coming back...

It was not required for her to mention who "she" is.

I knew it already.

Everyone did.

This is just the conformation.

Dear Dairy,

Thursday; 01/12

Firstly, I have been a lot busy these days. Learning script, translating it, studies, homework, pending classwork, the list goes on. It's been ten days since I got the conformation of Janes' leaving the school. Everyone has a different personality, characteristics, and comfort zone. This place just didn't suit her.

Secondly, a tragicomic event took place. Not "a" actually. A few. When it comes to the word "comedy" it's always Mateo.

Yesterday Mr. Aden took all of us to the lawn in front of the 5th grade. We sat on the grass and Mr. Aden asked Mateo to bring him a chair. He went in the 5th grade as the class was empty for some reason. When he got out, he was coming to say that

"sir! There is no cha–" vanished.

Mateo vanished in the middle of completing the sentence.

Everyone started laughing. Howling.

That's when I noticed, Mateo fell in the gutter between the walking path and lawn. The gutter is deeper than his height and that's how he vanished and as a matter of fact, *that* is the deepest gutter in the campus. The other guys were literally rolling on the grass while trying to control their laugh.

Later that day, Mr. Aden had another lecture with us after lunch break. Everyone had lunch faster than expected and we came to the class. The time was up and this time Mr. Aden called us to the smart class. It is a little 2-minute walk from our class but no one was paying attention to the time.

I was the first to leave the class. Kinsey followed me.

There is a pond in front of our class also, there is a gutter in the middle of walking path and the pond. The gutters are everywhere in the campus for avoiding water cloggage in rainy season as the campus is situated in middle of forest in an open space.

Me and Kinsey were walking and crossed the pond area. I heard a splash. I turned.

Ethan, Trevor, and Cyrus were standing in front of the pond but, their heads were facing the pond.

Cyrus gasped.

I looked in the pond. All I could see was white water lilies, pink lotus, leaf's everywhere and a head.

Mateo.

His head "on" the water, his body "in" the water.

Ethan laughed. Everyone laughed. Me and Kinsey dying on the walking path in the middle of campus.

"ETHAAANNN" Mateo screamed spreading his arms wide for Ethan to drag him out but, Ethan was busy dying due to laugh.

People get panic attacks; we were getting laugh attack.

Mateo called again and Ethan decided to help him out. Ethan grabbed the border between the pond and gutter from one hand, giving the other one to Mateo. Ethan caught him but due to the slippery surface, water touched his ankles. He pulled Mateo out.

Mateo was covered in algae and some lotus leaves. He looked exactly like a person should look after being tossed in the god-knows-when-cleaned pond. Everyone said he lost balance and fell but, I had my suspicion on Ethan as he was smiling like some who would toss a person in the god-knows-when-cleaned pond.

Mateo ran towards the hostel to get changed before any teacher finds out. God not being in his favour, we saw the most dangerous teacher heading in our direction. Chemistry teacher. Science students always said he has a bad temper. He slapped Bryan and Ezar once.

To avoid him, Mateo took a short cut which was jumping directly in the back side of our class and straight to his hostel rather than going all towards the dinning all and then turning to the long route of boys hostel.

I saw Mr. Aden coming from the smart class, he waved at us and pointed to the class. We all headed back towards the class and when I was two steps behind Mateo, he fell.

AGAIN.

This time he fell in front of the class door as he was bare foot and the floor was slippery. His crocs were floating in the pond.

I had a laugh attack again. Everyone did.

Chapter 17

"Do Not Tell, okay?" I make sure. "Yes, okay" she winked. Yesterday I was having fever at night. I am sick in every alternate week, God knows *WHY*. I didn't go to the doctor because I had a plan in my mind, I can't afford to miss more classes and she would have given me the same medicine she gives me every time but, I never take it.

I took my bag and hide it under the teachers table in our class with me. My plan is to see everyone's reaction when the big day is in a week and the "host" goes ill. Although we have a serious issue that I can barely speak right now due to throat infection but hot water will do its work later.

Fun is priority.

"Good morning!" Ezar greeted Kinsey as he entered and I could hear his footsteps leaving the classroom.

The wooden table was close from three sides and the open side is faced towards the board. The marble top is easily removable but strong. I am fitting perfectly inside.

"Hey!" Bryan came in.

A thud.

More thudding sound.

Wait… did he just sit on ~~my head~~ the table? He did.

He is sitting on the table and swinging his legs while they crash to the table and make my ears bleed with thudding. They talked for a bit and just when he was leaving the class he asked

"Where is Olivia?" in his usually normal tone.

"She is in the medical wing" Kinsey replied in a concerning tone.

"OH NO! everything is DONE now!" he exaggerated and left.

Henry stepped in the class the first thing he asked is where am I. Kinsey replied the same in the same plastic tone.

"Someone inform this to Mr. Scott! THE DAY is now in god's hands." He always got on my nerves and this exaggeration added to the list.

Mateo entered "it's okay, she will recover soon."

Ethan came in "who is sick?"

"Olivia" all three of them said at the same time.

"Bro what the hell happening?" and his footsteps faded.

I am laughing at their reactions. After everyone left for assembly. I got out, took a long breath, and went to the assembly hall. Everyone looked shock after seeing me here.

"I heard you were sick?" Ethan asked as I was passing him to grab my seat. Expressionless. Suspicious.

"I. Am." I managed to speak in my horrible voice.

"Got it, don't say another word otherwise my ears might die from horror" he confirmed my condition.

After lunch break, the classes are replaced with Founders' Day practice time. We are allotted the assembly hall for practice. As everyone is dancing, I am the DJ. I play, pause, and change the song according to their dance steps. They are dancing on two different songs one of which is choreographed by the choreographer hired.

This time is given to practice that part and whenever the choreographer is free, she will keep adding more to the progress. However, the part that is completed till now was to be performed in the morning assembly in next two days.

After a long day, me and Kinsey returned to our hostel after dinner. Played UNO with some seniors and some juniors. Back to bed.

Dear Dairy,

Sunday; 04/12

After coming from today's practice, we watched a movie. This time Saturday was for junior's movie, ours shifted to Sunday afternoon. Worst time for a movie. Sunday afternoons were always hectic and reserved for work.

Saturday nights were best movie timing as we just go and sleep. Anyway, after coming back from todays' show, I washed my cloths and two pair to shoes. I washed shoes for the first time in my life. I am proud of myself for making them brand new white, though I will be much more careful for not getting them dirty again. We are performing tomorrow in the morning assemble. I have my part ready.

Wish me luck!

Chapter 18

Its only three days left for the big day and all of us are sitting in the middle of main stage. WHY? Nobody knows.

Mr. Scott started going mad and made everyone around him mad too, including all of us. We were supposed to sit on the stairs of amphitheatre and wait for our turn to perform. Instead, Mr. Scott called us on the stage just to sit on the floor in the middle while other class performs in the corner.

Our class had a small act in the beginning and the dance in the ending, me and Trevor are hosting.

Now that we are here, while the performers in the corner are having the first part in the show are going with their practice, Ethan started to tickle Mateo.

None of these guys can sit quietly for too long.

The whole school is sitting right in front of us and we are currently the centre point of attraction. If these idiots won't do anything, how are we calling ourselves 11th graders?

Mateo laughs.

Cyrus starts to pass comments "look at that guy in the corner, the one in blue shirt. He looks gay."

"Are you nuts?" I ask, even though I know he is.

"Hell yes, I am, and look at the way that girl in green is standing. She is going to fall from trauma." Cyrus is not stopping.

Ethan joins him. Everyone starts to laugh. Luckily the amphitheatre is open and huge. Others could barely tell what we are talking about. Just when I am called to perform, a student in the previous acts goes missing.

When she is called and dragged from the last corner of the campus, mikes are not working.

Once that is fixed, Jay starts to stammer on his part. That wasn't funny though.

Now that todays' practice in amphitheatre is done, we go to the dance room after lunch. Ms. Jannet the Choreographer joined us for further dance steps. As I am not dancing, I carried my 15 pages script everywhere with me. Jay and Trevor are with me in the anchoring but they both had equally divided parts where as I am the permanent anchor.

The dance room has store/changing room one on the left the other on the right corner of the front wall. Side walls and back wall had big windows and the front wall is covered by a huge mirror.

Ms. Jannet is thinking for some steps just when I see Henry going in the store room in the right side. It is never locked. The other one is never open. Henry brought two tridents and passed one to Ethan, other to Mateo.

I could spot Cyrus sitting "on" the wall of the same store room. How did he get up there? I asked myself. He is wearing ghungroos in one leg which is a musical anklet used by performers in classical dance.

The wall of both store rooms is open from the top. Like an office cabinet for co-workers in big offices. Trevor is having a long piece of pipe with him. Bryan had a plastic jar which he attached to the pipe and acted as if he is having a camera.

Ethan and Trevor are fighting with their props and said they are playing fortnight. Then suddenly Jay jumped between them with a new pipe. It looked like Ethan seriously wants to murder him.

"We are making Incredibles 3!" Ethan shouted to get everyone's attention.

This scenario in front was me is an unexplainable disaster. Bryan is the camera man, Trevor is now directing and not leaving any opportunity to hit someone by hiding behind them, flying pipes crashing to the windows, Ethan bleeding from the lips, Trevor broke a toe nail and Mateo got a bruise on his leg, me and Kinsey having the biggest laugh attack.

Once everyone is done hitting each other and getting hit by each other, the practice resumed. After an hour, we are called to the amphitheatre again for the run-through.

The run-through took our whole evening and some of my friends already left for dinner while some are still practicing.

Me and Kinsey left for dinner and spotted Ethan and Mateo ahead us. The dining hall is empty, except us four and one student in the last corner. There are three food counters, one for boys, one for girls, and one for teachers. Now that the dinner time is almost over, only one counter is open.

We go there and server ourselves. Every class has a table allotted to them. One table for boys and one for girls. Our table is two tables away from the guys' table. As the whole place is empty, we joined the guys.

I kept my plate on the table in front of Ethan and Kinsey sat in front of Mateo just when Ethan started shaking his head.

"don't sit here, don't sit here, don't sit here, don't sit here, d-" barely audible and not even once looking up from his plate he kept repeating.

"Why?" I asked confused.

"You can't, it's not allowed and you already have a table allotted." He replied, still concentrated on his food.

"I know but each table is for 20 people, will it not be odd if we go and sit in the middle of 16 big tables? Just the two of us?" I made a point.

"It will be odd but you have to." Ethan said shoving some rice in his mouth.

We left them sitting in the middle of an empty dining hall and shoved our food inside.

Chapter 19

Whole day is for practice. I grab the essential drawing stuff as I was told to make a program invitation card for our chairman.

The day is going exhausting already and Mr. Scott is making me even more crazy. Founders' Day is in next two days and he says the script has some changes. Turns out, not some but a new script is added to the old one. Whole eight new pages to learn.

I have started to think Mr. Scott brings this last time changes to annoy us. Every time.

I am sitting on the side bench in the assembly hall, giving the card a finishing touch. I don't know where everyone went. I am alone. I try to find Mr. Joe and found him and others in the teachers' staff room.

We left the school within next ten minutes. It was me and Jay who were representing our school and Mr. Joe is with us as our mentor. We crossed a rose field on our way, banana plantation, everything here is under our chairman only.

When we reached, sitting in the wating room we drank some freshly made fruit juice and saw people in the offices working.

A person escorted us to the Chairmans' office and when I stepped in, I introduced myself first and continued with the details. I am sitting exactly opposite to him and Jay is on my right.

His office is very minimalistic. A plain white table with his big iMac sitting on top right. It's a big room with very limited objects. Yet, I still feel small.

*****

Dear Dairy,

I use you to write hilarious and amusing times only so that once I'm old, I could come back to you and live this past once again. I write as much as I could just to capture and stop this lifetime. We are writers, we don't cry. We bleed on paper. Anyway,

There is this little act our class is performing. The teacher appointed for all the drama is a himself a dramatic man. He never appreciates anyone for the performance.

Just like yesterday he was mocking Jay for his stammering and lack of commanding voice.

He made Trevor Walk in 50 different styles just to teach him to walk a little human like. Trevor really walks like a turtle.

Ezar and Henry always had a different pronunciation for some words which needed to be fixed. He made them repeat those words whenever they were trying to take some rest.

He wanted me to be loud during the anchoring and always asked me that how will I speak if the mics are not working?

Unfortunately, I was too loud that he made me practice to be loud but not louder. Whereas there is a very small role of an old and bold lady for Kinsey which had to be heard loud and clear. Kinsey has a voice one could barely hear sitting next to her.

Cyrus is always in a hurry and playing his role faster than required. He is learning to be little normal. Rest other things are comparatively fine. This exhausting but fun.

A few days back, we were having a free class and this time the boys had another activity in their mind.

I was sitting on the cabinets in the left corner of our classroom. The space is enough to fit 6 to 7 people together. Kinsey joined me once she was back from the Juice break. Bryan was standing in front of us. We were discussing something about the act and anchoring.

I saw all the guys standing in front porch between both the 11th classes. Half of them were in front of science class and the other half were standing in front of commerce. I left my place to check what was happening and sat on the stairs outside the porch.

Ethan, Cyrus, and Mateo

V/S

Trevor, Jay, and Henry.

It was a fight.

Then my eyes watched the object in centre.

A Lip Balm?

I didn't like where my mind was going.

When they start, my though was proven correct.

Oh no... this was a freaking LIP BALM fight.

The one I see Ethan carry everywhere for everyone; they use it all the time during lectures.

The goal posts were class doors and the main rule was, no one will be using hands.

This was more like a lip balm football more than a fight. They were pushing and crashing each other like animals.

Wild.

After a while, the lip balm tube broke but no one noticed. Someone steeped on it. "Ewwwwwwww..." gross, after seeing my expression everyone noticed that lip balm was now all over the floor and the worst thing was, they all were barefoot.

P.S. – I received Janes' letter, got to reply to her soon.

*****

Tomorrow is THE Day.

I am wearing a Plain White T-shirt with my all-time favourite black sweatpants. I pull a denim jacket as its chilly outside.

We are already late for assembly and I also skipped breakfast just like any other day. Who eats some fried onions in breakfast?

Someone calls my name from behind me during the assembly. I turn and see my Mr. Brandon waving me to meet him in the other corner of the hall.

"Yes sir?"

"We are going to take a photo for the next editorial team, are you sure you will take in in this attire?" his expression not showing the disappointment his voice making me feel.

What editorial team? What photo shoot? What is all this? And WHY was I not informed about this earlier?

Instead, I ask "what should I wear sir, I am sure I can quickly change and come before the assemble ends."

"Wear something semi-formal and decent. The photo will be used throughout the year." He looks bit more satisfied after my reassurance.

I run quickly to the hostel. I wear a simple sea green top with wine trousers and my casual white shoes. Luckily, I reach the assembly hall on the last note of our national song.

I spot Trevor, Ethan, and Cyrus looking at me and waving me to follow them.

"Care to explain?" I ask them.

"Just a photo of the editors." Trevor replies, his face as always stoned.

By all this fuss and the people trying to take our photo standing in front of me I confirmed that we are the new editors for our school magazine.

"You go there."

"You go there."

"No. you stand there."

"Guys what the hell?" after a ton of shoving each other, the decided the all three of them will stand one the right side of the statue and I will stand alone on the left.

They clearly want to stand away from me but no one is saying that out loud. They were just shoving each other until Ethan asks "Can't we all stand together, let her be there."

"No, you can't. one of you must come this side." Raquel says. She was one of the editors till now.

Trevor decided to join me because Ethan and Cyrus won't leave each other as bear to honey.

After this long drama. we had a proper run-through with costumes and spotlights till the night.

Recognise

Let your thoughts be wild
Don't burn them in the broad daylight

Don't compare yourself with sunshine and roses,
While you are completely orchids and moonlight

Darkness is nothing but absence of light
Shine bright high in the sky

They say recognition comes from time,
Keep your head high and let them recognise

Chapter 20

THE DAY.

Everyone is excited to see their parents. Wearing nice clothes for photos, the winter season is already setting the perfect cozy atmosphere. Most of the parents are here already, except mine.

Kinsey's parents have also arrived and I call my mom to get their update. One hour to go.

Mr. Scott won't leave me alone. He wants me to stick to his side and keep revising the script even though I am sure I am well prepared.

Ethan is sitting outside our class with his family, Trevor is walking around the campus with his, Mateo and his sister are standing close to Ethan, Ezar is busy catching his little brother who wants to run everywhere.

"Someone is calling you" a junior came to me as I am standing close to the pond.

"Who?" I ask.

"I don't know, she is a parent sitting outside the admin office" he says.

Kinsey's parents were sitting outside the office last time I saw them. I run straight towards to office. My woollen Sweater is making me sweat.

I spot Kinsey and her mother sitting together.

"You called me?" I manage to say catching a breath.

"Yeah, your mom called. They are entering the campus." She spoke.

FINALLY!

I already knew where they cars were going to be parked so I didn't bother her asking where they might be.

"Can I come with you? Getting board for real." Kinsey asked just before I was going to rush like a rabbit. "Sure."

We reached near the cricket ground and I spotted my grandmother with- my brother? He was coming?

I looked at Kinsey for conformation that I am not the only one who can see him. "Yeah, that's him. I knew."

Huh? Knew? How?

Before I could ask, she said "Your mom told me to keep it a surprise. You're welcome." She giggled.

My rabbit energy is already low as we ran all the way here. I remember once or twice I was not able to reply and check my mails, Kinsey had called her parents for some work and kept asking her mother if there was any message from my mother.

We all had lunch together and it was time for me to change into my decided fit. Me and Kinsey left everyone and reached our hostel. Got dressed, took some photos, and rush back to the assembly hall where we told our parents to wait.

Kinsey went her way and I ran towards my mom who is already prepared with her makeup tools for me.

Mom did my makeup, changed my jewellery, watch, hair style and I'm all set. I asked them to find their place in the centre of amphitheatre so that while they record me, the video will be from an eye level. I went back to the stage and that's when the program started.

Opening with an orchestra, speeches, and awards.

When the main story started, I entered the stage and the mic in my hand felt like my source of power. My golden dress shining bright from the spotlights. My light brown hair matching my big brown almond eyes.

I could feel my parents gaze on me along with hundreds of other parents. The spotlights were so bright that all I could see was black empty space.

I was a little nervous at first but, as the program carried on, my nervousness fled away.

There are so many things going all together I could barely keep a track of time and in the blink of an eye, the program ended.

Dinner arrangements are done in the football field. So many stalls. I took some photos with my friends and had dinner with my beloved family. After a whole month.

After dinner all the parents were gone. I hugged everyone and cried a little too much in seeing them off.

*****

Half of the school went home along with their parents as there is a school trip going. The ones not going are allowed to go home for the week. I am one of the trip packs.

This is going to be my first and last school trip ever. I have never been to a school trip before, for a week and no school takes the senior most class to long trips.

Its only me, Kinsey, Jay, and Henry now in class as others already left last night. Three different trips are going. The first to go is junior boys, second is senior boys, and third is all girls.

Dear Dairy,

I was super busy after Founders' Day was done. First packing, then the train journey, the whole trip, everything happened really fast.

Let's recall the bits and pieces I remember from the trip.

Firstly, the campus is in the forest on the outskirts of Janes' hometown. My mother informed her about the trip and train timings so she brought some food for the journey to the station as I was having very limited stock.

we reached our first destination, and the first day was all reserved for historical tours. Also, my parents brought me a camera for the trip as phones were not allowed. Camera was also not allowed but I got the permission on some conditions like at night it will be with the coordinating teacher and after going back to school, all photos will be transferred to the school for the record.

I didn't have any issue with all those things.

The next day we went to a different city where we were allowed some pool time in the hotel. This hotel was more like a private rental place with their staff. This day was mostly spent in travelling by bus.

The next morning, our third day was reserved for jungle safari and other wild life activities. That place was freezing cold. We were in the middle of the country's most dense forest. We also went to a souvenir store.

The fourth day we were taken again on another historical tour of that city. After getting back and already tired, we were provided noodles as snack. Worst noodles I ever had in my life.

The last day, that was the day when we were returning, in breakfast there was the world's most gross pasta. I skipped it off-course.

The bus took a halt at another souvenir store and that's when I purchased some stuff like a stone necklace, tiger printed T-shirt and some fridge magnets. That's all, I think. We reached the station hours later and got back to school the other morning.

Chapter 21

It's funny how things turn out when you don't want them to be that way. After I came back from the excursion many things have changed. When I went to class today it felt empty. Ethan and Bryan went for badminton matches in some other city. Trevor is not back from home. It is only Kinsey, Cyrus, Mateo, and me in the class.

Though the class felt empty, we enjoyed a lot. The guys always used to play 'pen fights' in their free time and I did nothing but observe them, it was fun to watch the games they used to play. I always wanted to play it but never got a chance.

Today is my opportunity to join Cyrus and Mateo as it is only two of them. Once me and Kinsey joined them, they taught us the strategies and it is fun somehow even if we are bad at it.

Then we played red hands so much that my right hand had a big blood clot on the top. I don't know what wrong I did to Cyrus in his previous life but he hits me like he is taking revenge from the past.

*****

Ethan and Trevor are back now and we all are having more good times as the days are passing.

All of us have made such a bond that it's hard to imagine a class without these people. I even started hating Bryan less as he is not being a jerk and actually trying to be friends.

Rumour has it today is the raid day. Students bring a lot of stuff after coming from the trip. The checking is done on the main gate itself before entering the premises but, everyone knows the trick to hide the tuck. What's much funnier is that teachers are as smart as the students, they know that the tuck has entered the premises somehow. It happens every time.

Once the raid is done, they take away all the illegal food items but sometimes... some kids get away with it.

Including us.

Today during lunch time, the students were all running to their dorms skipping the meal. That's when I got to know about the raid. I had some chocolates which are lying on the top of my suitcase.

Me and Kinsey managed to hide the stuff temporarily.

The danger is not gone.

At night, We are sitting in Sarah's room and everyone is there. A security guard comes inside the room without knocking. The security lady asked us to submit all the stuff we had or else she would take it herself. Grace eyed us to go to our room.

She whispered "Just give one fourth of whatever you have, she needs to believe we gave whatever we had." Grace made a point.

I gave a few chocolates and biscuits from my side and Kinsey is clean. Genuinely. She is always out of trouble as she bought a jar of Nutella and a few chocolates *only once*. Whereas I am full of illegal food stuff. The illegal includes coffee, chocolates, biscuits, and every packaged food. Nothing less.

The security lady checked our wardrobes just for the sake of her satisfaction. My bag of chocolates is kept right on the top of the shelf and when she touched it, I thought my life ends here and now.

Her phone rang. She ignored it.

It rang again.

She took it.

Thanks to the person who called her just in the perfect time and she left me and my stuff alone. Kinsey let out a big sigh of relief as we just came out of the deaths' jaw right before being swallowed.

The next morning is quiet. No raid rumours going around. The day has just started. Just when I entered the class, I heard someone say "girls are the next target, they took our stuff yesterday and today it's their turn."

Not again…

as soon as the lectures ended, I ran to the dorm and checked if everything was fine.

Just in time I saw Blair hiding her stuff in her room.

"Are girls the next target?" I asked her as if I couldn't believe it even after watching her hiding her stuff in a hurry.

"Girls? You really believe it?" what a reli-

"it's us bro. We are the targets. The senior most are the most suspicious ones. Welcome to reality" she dropped the bomb.

Reloading……

Processing……

Updated.

DAMN IT.

Her words left me deep in my darkest dreams. I must do my best to cover up the mess or else these are my last days here.

It's already 3 A.M. and me and Kinsey are going to execute our plan. We planned a lot of tricks which were the best ones but ended up using someone's advice everyone would do the opposite off. Freaking Linda.

Scissors, check.

Needle, check.

Thread, check.

Tape, check.

Lights off.

We. Are. Ready.

Step 1: tear it from the middle. Done.

Step 2: stick all the drugs inside. It took us an hour but, done.

Step 3: stitch the part and you are completely safe.

Well, I won't say completely safe but quite relieved that now my treasure won't be found until and unless someone holds the mattress vertically. I made sure that there is no sound coming from the packets after Kinsey is sleeping on it but, if someone tries to press it intentionally the packets are making a little sound which without any doubt will get us suspended.

The mattress had two different layers which were stuck to each other with glue. I tore it apart and stuffed the drugs inside and for extra safety, I taped everything together.

As we couldn't leave that whole part open for everyone to enjoy our treats and efforts, I had to stitch it up completely. Kinsey knows nothing of stitching. I got to know this after cutting the mattress cover. It was almost morning and we slept for an hour just to stay alive in the classes next day.

It is a matter of ten days and we are going home. I don't understand the concept of raiding currently.

WHY?

Bloom

Life isn't a fairy tale
Even barbies are bored of this game

Challenges maybe Challenging
Living like fragile flowers won't be entertaining

Aim for the best
but give up the 'rest'

Success isn't about making money
But being satisfied with your life honey

Be who you are
Bloom with the scar

Stitch all the wounds up and show them your real power

Chapter 22

New year brings new opportunities, new goals, new hopes, new targets, new desires, and everything new. This is my first new year which I celebrated in school and hopefully it will be my most memorable time.

In this school we organise a commerce fest during the last 3 days of December.

This is one of the biggest events celebrated here.

Commerce fest starts on 29th December and ends by 31st December. Every year students of class 11th are the organisers.

On 29th, the first day of commerce fest, we organise the assembly. The assembly is based on our theme and the inauguration of commerce fest.

This year the theme is based on the development of rural to urban. The backdrop is painted by us and all the materials required are provided by the art department.

The drawing of huts and agriculture is connected to a bridge showing how things developed and transformed. In the form of buildings and technology we showed urbanisation.

Trevor and Kinsey went to the market to get the decoration stuff. Meanwhile, I oversaw the backdrop. I was guiding how to paint and where to paint.

Some of the juniors really pissed me off and Ethan asked them to leave before I could show them what it is like to test my patience.

I am busy making the invitation card for the chief guest for the inauguration.

In the meantime, someone got painted, someone spilled the paint water on the stage. Someone was so hungry that they ate four plates of pasta and so many more funny parts.

Our target is to complete the backdrop today itself. Tomorrow is going to be the first day of the 'commerce fest.'

I don't carry my wardrobe key with me all the time. Today I carried it in my bag. I kept my laundry last night but forgot to give a red T-shirt hanging on the chair.

I am wearing the most printed top I have which my mom accidently got for me. It's filled with tiny yellow, red, and orange flowers.

Today onwards, there will not be academic classes at least till the new year begins.

I am called in the middle of painting to the staff room. Mr. Aden said I am going to the chief guest's house to invite them. He asked me to change into something decent. I made the card but didn't think I would be the one going to hand it over.

I ran towards the dorm. Again. Whenever I am trying to wear something more comfortable, something urgent and "decent" comes up.

Got out of this un-decent top.

'Oh shit!' Realisation hit me right at my head that my backpack is in the assembly hall. My wardrobe key is in the side pocket of it.

Luckily this red T-shirt lying on my chair saved me, I changed into it as it is impossible to button the top again.

I started running towards the assembly hall to get my keys.

Henry shouted when I crossed him in front of the dining hall, "don't go in those clothes."

I know you idiot. I quietly ignored him and continued.

"Are you crazy?! You cannot come in that! Go and change it now." says the guy in blue from head to toe.

Who else would be this over smart other than Ethan. He himself.

When I reached the assembly hall, Bryan is standing beside my backpack. I ask him to throw the key and that idiot came running half way and just when he was just about to reach me, he rolled them towards me. Before he would comment on my outfit, I gave him the details.

I changed into a pastel pink top with the same navy-blue pants. This is the most decent shirt I own.

I went back to the staffroom and waited for Ethan.

He arrived and we left.

When we reached the guests office, it is huge. The cabins for all the workers are separated with walls made of glass. We were told to wait as the person is in a meeting.

The waiting cabin is small, Mr. Joe is sitting across from us and he is discussing the business of this company with us.

General knowledge he says.

One of the employees knocked on the door. Ethan got up and took the juice bottles from his hands. Their business is fresh juices. They even run this school. So basically, we are here to invite the youngest son of the founder of the school.

Once we are in his office, I introduce myself and our theme of this year for the commerce fest. Ethan goes on with the details.

Once we are back from there, my fantastically dumb teammates have a new task for me. I feel like hitting each one of them with Thor's hammer.

Cyrus brings me a ton of chart papers and the plan is to write around forty quotes by some known personalities on each of them.

These are to be pasted on every pillar in sight from the assembly hall all the way till the dining hall. I started with cutting the sheets into half.

Bryan and Mateo join for help. As they are cutting, I am writing.

I nearly completed thirty posters; it is dinner time. After dinner, girls are not allowed to stay for a longer time. The backdrop painting is finished and it is looking awesome.

*****

Next morning, we were told to arrive at the assembly hall at sharp five. Me and Kinsey carried the poster stuff with us. It is so exhausting to shower early in the morning and we were the first to leave the dorm.

Even the security guard was watching us to see what we are up to.

The school never felt so empty.

The trees are silent. Winds are rushing through the empty paths. It felt like I am the only one here. It was a sense of loneliness, I thought but, it was something different, more like a sense of relief.

I spread my tools on the stage and started the work.

After an hour and half my classmates Showed up. Each one of them are in formals. Trevor gave me some stickers with our company name printed on them. I completed the remaining quotes and handed them to Kinsey and Bryan.

They went to paste the posters on the pillars while I helped others in the final touch. Kinsey and Mateo are the hosts. This is the first event in the school in which I did not have any part. This is the time for me to sit and enjoy. For once.

The chief guest arrived at the main gate and the host went missing. Mr. Aden started to panic and asked me to host it. Ethan asked me to find Kinsey and Bryan while he is assuring the teacher that if they are not here, I will be hosting.

I searched the whole School but could not find them. Cyrus came to the dining hall and called me. "Sir is very angry; you are going to host." he Informed me and both of us went back to the assembly hall. I took the script and started to revise it.

And I thought I will be the one enjoying it.

When we reached the Assembly Hall, I could spot Kinsey heading here. She arrived just in time as the chief guest is two blocks behind her. The program started, the cover on the backdrop was removed. Everyone could see our painting right now and I am feeling very embarrassed. To my surprise everyone liked that so much that we got a thunder round of applause.

The Assembly was a success, we had a photoshoot session and everyone is dispersed.

As we have a lot of work to do and there are no classes. In conclusion, it was time for more fun.

We return the stuff which is not required anymore to the art department. I am going to present a presentation in the assembly the next day and it is related to my entrepreneurship activity. Ethan and Trevor are also going to present on the same day.

One of the teachers took us to the Assembly Hall again to prepare the presentation. I was completely lost and forgot about the content in my presentation. Ethan somehow managed and fooled the teacher. He said the computer is not working so none of us should present.

In the evening, I went to the computer lab with Bryan and got the print outs of my presentation to prepare throughout the night. I mailed my parents and did a little bit of chit chat with them.

*****

On 30th December, that is the second day of commerce fest,

The three of us are going to present our Entrepreneurship presentation in front of the director. I am in complete formals. My black blazer is confusing most of the juniors with an outsider.

Once Ethan and Trevor are done, it is my turn. I had my presentation mailed to Ethan's ID as I didn't have one of my own. Turns out, he never received it.

That bastard Bryan.

I was using his ID till now and had the password to it. I asked him to mail it to Ethan so that it will be easy for me to open it on the big screen. This was weeks ago.

Panic rushing in my veins. All eyes on me.

After a long 10 minutes which felt like the worst 10 hours of my life, my stuff was on the screen.

When I went on the stage, I am blank. I had the content in front of me and I got completely blank.

Firstly, my presentation was not opening and next is when it did, I got so anxious that I forgot half of my preparation.

After I completed my part, I am feeling very uneasy.

The director stopped me before leaving the auditorium.

"What happened to you? Are you the same person who set fire to the stage on Founder's Day? You could have done better. This was not expected from you, especially." this is all she said.

I felt very humiliated though, the way she said this was very kind and for my own benefit. I stomped towards the hostel, removed my blazer in anger and tugged my shirt out furiously. When I reached my room, I busted into tears with the constant flowing guilt inside me.

Though we got to learn many new things from those presentations, it helped us a lot in general knowledge and our Entrepreneurship marks were supposed to be given on the way we presented it. I was in the class all day after that and was busy painting the invitation card for the funfair. I am supposed to complete the card before lunch.

I am lost in completing it, I lost track of time. Everyone is already in the dining hall and when I stepped out of my class there is Ethan's family sitting all over the trees.

Me and Kinsey went back inside the class and checked if there is any way they would jump on us. We waited here for almost 15 minutes when we saw the principal heading towards the dining hall. We explained the situation to him, we got the most unexpected and the most unhelpful answer according to the situation.

"Even I am afraid of Monkeys...." He spoke.

how are we supposed to go for lunch then? The principal spotted a junior heading our way and called him.

"You are our only opportunity and only help to cross the path." he said to the little boy who is almost 4 years younger than us.

The little guy leads and we are hiding behind him like the monkeys won't be able to spot our huge bodies from the trees they are hanging on.

When we reached, 12th graders performed a street play in front of the dining hall. They showed different colours of water, how water is used for wrong purposes like using acid to settle scores, depletion of water causing damage to farmers, And so much more.

When I went to the Mr. Aden with the card, he hated it.

He is already in a bad mood and my card just pissed him more. He scolded me for at least a half an hour or so. I am on the edge of my limit. The day is a complete mess.

I stomped towards the 12th class, as it is empty and right next to the admin area, I started to make a new card. The next card I made is very simple. I made some floral designs around the circle in the centre which was hollow to reveal the content of the card. This is much better as compared to the one I made before, using so much colour paper and making it look childish.

This one looked like a mature person made it, it looked like how exactly it should have been in the first place.

Mr. Aden asked me to invite the chief guests again but, this time I had no other option but to deny the offer. I badly wanted to talk to my parents as this day is going really crappy.

I called my parents the second after the students were sent for the invitation. I cried very badly on the call. When I started to cry after my mother picked up, she thought something serious happened to me. Then after a perfect ten minutes of call, I got out of the booth, crying again.

Kinsey asked me to sit on the stairs in front of the small waterfall at the entrance. It is only the two of us when Ezar, Bryan and Jay were crossing. They saw me crying and stopped for a brief hour.

I am glad I am wearing a mask, the mucus pouring out from my nose and the tears are all on my face and it is very gross.

*****

31st is the last and the most exciting day of commerce fest, last day of the year. Students of class 9th presented a presentation in the assembly. This day is the most awaited day in school. We arranged a comedy show in the auditorium after snacks and after that it is time for the most enjoyable part of the event,

The FUN-FAIR!

We are preparing for the funfair for rest of the day. From pumping balloons to arranging games. The total number of games are 9 and made by students of class 9th commerce section under the guidance of members of class 11th.

Decorating the art block is so fun. The wall hanging is sticky from one side to stick to the wall but, the wall we are going to attach it too, is made of uneven stones. I got a rope and started to attach it to the wall handing so that the rope can be tied to the nails in the wall.

Ethan helped me in that. Him and Mateo Fixed it to the wall.

Jay is making chits for the musical tombola alone. Me and Kinsey hopped on the side of him and started cutting the sheet into tiny pieces.

There is a creep in my class whom I hated the most, he was good for nothing in my opinion. This is the very first time I found him useful as he is making balloon bunches for the entrance.

Everyone has their own talent.

Everyone is enjoying the fuss. Mr. Aden is taking pictures of everyone doing their work. The people who are not doing anything are also busy with the photoshoot.

We had already distributed work to the juniors a few days back. They are supposed to make games using cardboards, paper sheets and everything available in the art department.

To our surprise they did a really fine job. There are many interesting games like basketball throw, ball toss, maze ball and many more.

We all are wearing our UNIMOS Merchandise. All the 9th graders had our t-shirts but, only the organisers had Bomber jackets. The t-shirt is White and it had our logo printed on it with our company's tagline on the back.

The jackets are also cool. Black jackets with white print, black pants, and white shoes.

All of us looked like a music band.

It's show time!

As we are the organising department we are roaming here and there, keeping an eye on our juniors, and guiding them. All of us enjoyed ourselves to the fullest.

The thought of after party hovering my head 'tasty food for once.' We have also planned for a special dinner tonight. Everyone will have different stalls to handle and the best part is its all random unhealthy and tasty menu. Once in a year opportunity for everyone to stay in this place and eat heavenly food.

When the fun fair started, all of us are enjoying a different vibe. Everyone is so colourful it was hard to identify them. None of the games are for free. Everyone Carried a coupon with them in which the amount with the game they are playing is mentioned. The shiny wall hanging side is used as a photo corner. We even had a lot of props for the photos of New Year eve.

Me and Jay are handling the music system. When I am talking to Jay, someone punched me in the head. I turned around. Found no one.

I could see Mateo laughing like he would after doing something he shouldn't have done.

Mateo has never dared to touch me even in a friendly way, Bryan and Cyrus were the only people who hit me whenever they wanted on the head. Just for fun of course. When I checked the photo corner, Bryan is busy already, taking pictures of someone and Cyrus is with the seniors.

I am very furious but, I let it slide for the time being. when I told Jay he asked me to leave it but, this time that person is not going to escape. The funfair went on till the late evening.

After that, all of us ran towards the lawn as we had duty on the food counters. When I am alone on my food counter Mateo asked me if I needed any help. I blasted.

"How dare you touch me?!"

He started to fight back as expected.

"What are you talking about? I didn't do anything"

is he an idiot or does he take me as an idiot?

"If you ever touch me again, I swear I am not going to hold back. We are not friends that you are so free with me. Be in your limits" I said standing close enough to grab him by the collar and throw a punch at his face.

Before he could say anything, others arrived and he quietly moved to his counter. My counter is full of rush as I am selling mango smoothies.

When I am standing alone and a group of people came pushing each other, It is hard for me to manage everyone on my own. Bryan is roaming here and there. When he saw the rush, He came to help me.

Meanwhile Cyrus is popping out of nowhere with a handful of Garlic Bread and a mouth full of pastry.

We were instructed to not eat anything until the event is about to end. After watching Cyrus I had a good opportunity to mock him.

"Let me call a teacher, someone is violating the rules" I smirked.

"Sve me sum, I wil com back lator." He is barely making sense with that pastry in his mouth. Bryan went to the stall next to us which had yummy Cheese balls and Paneer Tikka handled by chef Jay.

He returned with a single cheese ball and half piece of paneer and shoved them in my mouth.

"I thought we are not allowed to eat." I said while trying to take all the flavours at once.

"No by ourselves, but we have no other option when someone else feeds us." He winked. Valid point.

Bryan is feeding everyone in our group and that's when the teachers said at last, "you won't get time to eat, start eating before you starve yourselves all night."

After everything is finished, we packed up the stalls, helped the workers in cleaning the mess. One of the helpers signed me towards the last table which is left untouched and whispered something which I am not able to understand at all.

When I got a little closer all I could see is two heads and four legs. By the two pairs of shoes, I could tell those are of Ethan and Cyrus.

They are sitting under the table. When I went a little closer, I could see a plate in their hands.

Garlic bread.

These huge monkeys are hiding from everyone and enjoying the garlic bread all to themselves. I sat down with them, had a piece and this is the first piece of garlic bread I had this year. The cheese is not perfect, the amount of garlic is not up to the mark but still, I enjoyed it like anything.

They asked me to call the rest of the people of our group so that all of us could have at least a piece. Eleven people sitting under a table which cannot even adjust two plates on it, were enjoying every bite of the garlic bread. Kinsey had some pastries left from her counter so it is not only garlic bread but the pastries too.

After enjoying every single bite of the meal all of us went to the assembly hall as the public is waiting for the organisers to come and start the musical tombola.

Two members are going to the teachers to pick the chits and according to that the songs are being played. The songs were very refreshing. Selected by Trevor, he has a great taste in music.

A proper mix of classical, hip hop and pop, the crowd is getting energetic from time to time.

There are many winners too who received the gifts.

The night is very exhausting and very memorable. We enjoyed it to the fullest and as the game ended the commerce fest is also done. We did a little photoshoot session with Mr. Aden and our group. once we are done, all of us are sent back to the hostels.

I got to learn many different strategies of management throughout the fest and it helped in increasing my knowledge. Not only did I learned many things but also after spending so much time together in teamwork, I created a new bond with everyone. The main purpose of organising the commerce fest is to learn and enjoy to the fullest. Last but not the least, it was a very joyful and refreshing start to a

HAPPY

NEW

YEAR!

Chapter 23

Someone is knocking on the door. The music is too loud. Someone is talking very loudly. The beats of the music are very irritating. Someone started shouting and before my ears bleed, I open my eyes.

It happens every Sunday. As this is the only day I sleep for hours. I skip breakfast every time and if I'm caught sleeping during breakfast time, it's my house parents' glare and my world would come to an end.

I have tried to explain to her many times that my sleep is much more important than the breakfast I will probably skip after looking at it just like every other day but she won't listen.

Kinsey has also adopted my routine and we both sleep till noon. Today the music is irritatingly frustrating. The worst of its type. How can someone even call it music? To make it the perfect definition of one of the most annoying mornings, the house parent is shouting like anything and the music won't end.

I got up, brushed my teeth, changed my clothes, and went to the dining hall. Breakfast time is already over and gates of the dining hall are closed. I could spot Bryan and Henry standing in front of the gate. Kinsey catches up with me while we go to them.

"And look who is here just in time" Henry looked quite relieved to see us whereas the lines on Bryan's forehead is showing the tension.

"What did you do to Mateo yesterday?" Bryan's first sentence was the last thing I would want to hear in the already messed up morning. Especially the last name I would talk about in life.

Before I could say anything, I noticed that he is asking the question to Kinsey, not me. Now that looks like a wholly new topic.

She replied "I just told him to be in his limits"

I stop. What in the world are they talking about?

I said that to him.

How is Kinsey involved?

"What did he do?" Bryan asked calmly but, his face is showing otherwise.

"He kept his hands on my shoulder, and moved me from the position I was standing in the group photo. He is not a friend of mine to touch me like that." She explained glowering.

wow… The same person did the same thing with me and I said the same thing to that same person.

"And when were you going to tell me this?" I asked her slack-jawed.

"Both of us were so tired last night, I was going to tell you in the morning itself but because of the perfect morning, I stayed quiet." She replied facing me. Makes sense.

We were very tired and this was the last topic either of us would want to discuss. Bryan turns to me and gives me the same peering look he gave Kinsey before asking the question.

"And what did *you* do?" he asked.

"I just told him to be in his limits" I laughed a little then stopped.

Kinsey is looking at me wide eyed. She claps her hands to cover her mouth and to show the surprise on her face. Bryan shakes his head to come back to senses. Henry takes more interest in the conversation than before.

"When did *this* happen?" Kinsey looks at me with full of excitement in her eyes.

I give them the details and now both are looking at me in an unreadable expression. They are shocked. I could tell.

"Did he say anything?" Now me and Kinsey are focused on Bryan as WHY is he asking us this thing first in the morning.

"He was crying all night. Said 'the girls are only rude to me and no one else', he also added that both of you bad mouthed about him. Whatever, that brat deserves it." Bryan pressed his forehead by his palm.

I wished it was him standing in place of Bryan, I just want to slap him now that I have already missed the opportunity last night. While all of us are laughing at what happened yesterday, I could see Trevor approaching us.

"Let's go, Ethan and Cyrus are already waiting for us." Trevor informs.

"Where?" I asked in confusion.

"To clean the art block of course, did you thought it was going to clean itself?" he stomped off.

I never thought about anything.

"Or these guys never informed you that they were standing here and waiting for the two of you to come. What else can be expected from Bryan when it comes to girls." Trevor turns while walking and teased Bryan.

Everyone teases Bryan for talking to girls as he is friends with every girl in the campus. Half of the girl's population are not friends with me. More like enemies but, that's a different story. It's a whole new book.

We are standing in front of the art block and discussing who will clean which part. Suddenly the inner monkey of Bryan wakes and he climbs on the tree next to us. For real.

First, we started with taking out the colourful flags hanging in the middle of the art block from tree to tree. The place in the middle has a stone flooring and it has no shed. We used that part for the games. There are two corridors, one on each side of the open space. All the art and crafts activity classes are here. Then there comes the main wall which we used for the photo corner. That is the common wall between both the corridors and connects to the open space in the middle.

Next what we did is to take out the shiny wall hangings and keep it safe for farewell. The black and silver stripes were giving exactly new year's vibes. Then suddenly when I am busy popping the waste balloons, Cyrus and Ethan started to play with a tennis ball. Cyrus is in front of me, a few steps away and he is aiming at Ethan. Meanwhile Ethan is standing right in front of me.

Do they think I am this stupid?

Wherever I am moving, Ethan is following me. This confirmed my doubt. They are trying to hit me indirectly. I moved in front of Bryan who is busy talking with Jay. I waited for Cyrus to throw the ball and as he did, Ethan moved, I moved. The ball hit Bryan's butt.

He got up and started running towards Cyrus who is running like a horse. Me and Ethan are enjoying the run when the ball suddenly hit my head.

"You freaking rascal!" I shouted from far away as after hitting me, Cyrus knew I would settle the score.

He is now running for his life. Bryan is the one enjoying it now. As soon as I started to run, Cyrus fell down the step of the open space to the corridor. I am laughing and that's when I noticed he isn't.

He smiled languid.

I looked at his foot and it is bleeding. Turns out the thumbnail of his toe broke.

Ouch....

We stopped there and went back to the team. There is a black box kept in front of the wall. I am sitting in between Bryan and Kinsey. Trevor and Ethan are standing in front of us. Jay is sitting next to Bryan.

All of us are just making fun of last night's events.

The boys are doing some 'boys' gossip' and assuming me and Kinsey are not able to understand a single word.

Whereas only we know how we are holding our laughter in the whole time.

I never thought cleaning up after the fun would also be fun. After all of us were finally done, we packed everything in boxes and the boys took it with them.

*****

We had our exams which went the same as before.

Today was the last exam as well as the last day to go home.

Yesterday, I undid my hours of ~~handwork~~ hard-work and packed the stuff in my suitcase to take home as after that day the raid never took place. Also, Kinsey added insult to injury during dinner. She was walking to the plate wash area in front of me after we were done with fooling teachers that we had *proper* dinner. Just when we were about to cross the boys table, she tripped.

She slipped in a way one would think she did it purposely. Her plate was still in her hand be she dropped the glass. It rolled directly towards the chemistry teacher. Oh God this couldn't be any funnier. I rolled on the floor there itself instead of helping her to stand.

"don't look, don't look, for Christs sake don't look" she kept repeating looking at the backs facing us.

Bryan turned hearing the commotion. He started to tell everyone. One by one they all turned around and got a perfect picture of Kinsey and me still sitting on the floor, legs crossed and still laughing while the chemistry teacher is looking at us still confused what just happened. We laughed even after returning back to our hostel and pictured how the whole school might have looked at us while we just sat there like we were out of our minds.

Today, just when my parents arrived, I took some photos with everyone. It is a ten day leave but once all of us are back we would directly leave this place at the end of this session. End of this season.

"You can take photos some other time, it's not like you won't get the chance again."

That's what my father said but, who knew that would be our group's first and last photos.

Chapter 24

I feel happy to be back. Last ten days I enjoyed my time at home to the fullest. Once I am back in my dorm. It took me at least four hours to unpack my stuff.

It always takes *at least* four hours.

Days are going well. Our class had the strongest friendship I never thought would be. I had different views about everyone when I joined. I used to think Ethan and Trevor are full of themselves as they are the only oldies.

Cyrus is as warm as the sun, Mateo is as silly as fun, Bryan is as tall as a tree, Ethan is as scary as the sea, Trevor is always as cold as ice, Kinsey is as sweet as sugar and rest everything is nice.

This is the shortest description about everyone I could give at that time. Now things have changed, I found it wasn't hard to fit in. The more you talk to people the more you get to know them. I never give up on people until I try, try and try till I am tired of trying.

Today, *all* of us played red hands *together* for the first time. Pole to pole is a common game between us now.

Twelve people playing red hands, it was impossible to fit between their huge bodies but somehow me and Kinsey managed to squeeze in. The sequence is decided randomly.

Kinsey is trapped between Mateo and Trevor, whereas I am trapped between Ethan and Bryan. It is Bryan's turn to hit my hand. His hands are big, mine are small.

Ethan started adjusting my hand on top of his so that he won't be able to take the hit but, just as fast as Bryan's hand hit mine, Ethan's hand matched the speed.

It was Ethan's hand and Bryan's face.

Turned out that Bryan's long fingers had an impact on Ethan's hand as my hand is small so it took only a small hit.

This looked like a comedy scene from some movie.

After the tom and jerry run, everyone is tired.

"Hey OOlivi, pass me water" this is the most common dialogue I have heard Ethan say during classes.

I am the only one who carries a water bottle in the class, Ethan started the trend and now everyone drinks water from it. The bottle has my name engraved on it but that's the only thing mine to call, otherwise it belongs to the class.

I have even stopped to take it with me anywhere, it lies in the class always. The most irritating thing is they just drink the water and ask me every time to fill it.

If I'm thirsty and I fill it, either Cyrus or Ethan will snatch it from me, empty it and then thank me that I got water for them. First the water bottle and second the pens.

"Hey Ooolivi, give me a pen" no explanation needed about the beggar. He always asked for my pens and never ever returned a single pen back. This is so annoying for me and their source of entertainment during lectures.

Interhouse Badminton matches are starting tonight.

Me and Kinsey went before time to save the seats. There is a senior from my house who is an expert. He and Mr. Joe played together most of the time and their match are always interesting. Mr. Joe teaches us business studies and his classes are always fun.

In the semifinals Ethan and Brayn had a match. That was awesome. Watching them play was real fun.

When Ethan is on the side I am sitting, I cheered for him with all the energy I had. When they switched sides, I showed the same energy for Brayn.

Ethan and that senior had the final match and the senior won. The match just ended and people started spreading rumours that the senior said he won't play badminton ever again in his life if he loses this match and because of that Ethan played leniently.

I know how they both play as I have been observing them for months. I think Ethan would have made it if he wanted too. When the competition is about to end and everyone started leaving, Kinsey dragged me in the court again to congratulate both Ethan and Brayn for the energy they showed in the game and how well they played.

Chapter 25

"You are going to run, don't worry it won't be much"

is she crazy?

I have never participated in any race before as I know I'm not made for it. Linda just dropped a bomb on my head saying she gave my name to the house captain and assured him I will be running for at least a bronze.

"Can't I just take my name out?" I said trying not to hit Linda.

"No, you can't, you know.... There must be someone of your age group and you are the only one to fill that place." She speaks.

I was in my room. Sitting on my bed, minding my business when suddenly Linda busted into my room.

I. AM. DONE. FOR. SURE.

"I'm telling you this is a very very BAD idea." I insisted. Panic rushing in my blood.

"I don't have a choice, neither do you. I'm heading out first as I have my online class in a few minutes. Just go and practice daily and you'll cut through it." She completes and turns to leave.

What is this? Is it like making a tea or coffee that she is taking it so lightly, for me making tea or coffee is also complicated.

"When is the practice starting? And when is the sports day?" I ask just to be sure.

"Oh! That, the practices started in the last two days and the sports day is in next ten days from today." She left the door open as she matched towards the IT lab.

WHAT THE HELL IS WRONG WITH LIFE.

Where are my housemates? Dead probably

That's why they never got a chance to inform me. I'm already fifteen minutes late for the practice. I'll just go tomorrow.

"Oli... Oolivi.... OLIVIA!" Kinsey busted in the room.

"What's the matter, I'm not deaf. Stop shouting will y- woah, why are you sweating so much bro? Where are you coming from?" I look at her wide eyed. She is breathing so fast and looks like she'll fall by a small stroke of wind.

"I came running from the football ground all the way here because- because the coach is searching for you—- he wants you to participate in the school parade." She manages to speak while catching some air.

Her hands on the door handle, body bending forward.

A long pause.

I stare at her in confusion. Did the coach really ask for ME?

I don't think he even knows my name. And just in time Kinsey answers the questions I was about to ask her.

"He doesn't know your name but when he was asking if any other girl was capable of joining the parade." She stands straight.

"So, you gave my name?" I stare at her. Blank.

"Nope, I was not the one. A bunch of juniors. I don't think you'll be needing more explanation because we don't have time for this. He asked me to return in five minutes." She is standing still.

"You can leave now as you have already informed me." The look on her face answers my question that I am wrong. He didn't ask her to just INFORM me…

Oh god save me.

"He asked me to return *with* you. If you are not coming by yourself, I have no other option other than drag you because I can't let the energy go to waste if I go without you" she grabs my water bottle and passes me my joggers.

Great.

What else is left to go wrong? We run all the way to the football field as fast as we could.

Once I am here, I see a group of boys practising for the march past on the left and girls practising for the same on the right side of the football field.

The coach is on a break and he asked a junior to command the group. Her voice is so low that even after standing in the front row I am not able to hear her properly.

Just in time the coach returned with news that the one commanding the group now will be commanding on the final day too.

"I'm done with this" I say clenching my teeth.

I seriously am. We seriously are. Me and Kinsey looked at each other and without any explanation both of us were having the same thought.

"Let's talk with the coach" Kinsey stole words from my mouth and we went to the coach who is standing with the principal busy in discussing other fuss.

"Sir, can't you change the commander?" this is the first thing that came out of my mouth. I was thinking of doing some buttering first but what's said is said.

"Is her voice the problem?" he says without looking away from that girl. Sounds like he is aware of the problem too.

"Yes, we aren't able to hear a single command" I try to sound sincere rather than rude.

"Who do you want me to ask for the command then?" he asked.

This is unexpectedly expected.

"I can do it" words leave my mouth like an arow.

This is my chance.

"Okay, you will be the commander and Kinsey will be the captain then. Does this work?" he looks at us in genuine concern.

We nod and leave.

Wow! This is the best outcome without any buttering.

I asked the girl politely to shift her position.

It's a different thing that she created a lot of nuisances and started gossiping about us behind our backs but I did what I wanted to and her words doesn't cost a penny.

I have a loud voice and so does Bryan. I could hear him from the other corner of the open field.

Now that I am on the very front I can clearly see and listen how he is commanding which I should follow. Bryan is not selected for commanding, the seniors are but, as their exams are going on he oversees the practice.

The first day is hectic but it is worth it.

*****

Today the selections for field events are supposed to take place. Including long jump, disc throw and shot-put matches as the time won't be enough on sports day.

I am so very worried that today is the first day of my life I am going to run in a race. Even though it is a 100-metre run, I have never ever participated in running before. Thanks to Linda I'm stuck in this mess.

When I asked my house captain to remove my name from that race, he insisted so much that I ended up staying. Today it's different. I know it is. I know I can't do it.

What if I trip in the middle? What if I come at the very last? What if I fail? What will others think of me? How will my teammates feel?

What if I– wait.

Don't go there.

I am doing it no matter what. I have to do it no matter what.

My captain is guiding me how to stand so that I can get a better start.

I have to do it. Whatever happens I will not be demotivated.

3...2...1! bang!

I'm in everyone's line, I can make it. Just a little more.

No ...no..no..nononono my legs are not supporting me...

I'm going to lose... imaloser... I snapped back to reality and everyone is already ahead of me.

I stopped.

I would have covered a few participants but I just stopped.

I stupidly stood in the middle of the track.

And now, I am late.

Everyone has already reached and I am still standing in the middle. I started to leave the track from the middle but then someone yelled.

"Complete the race Olivia" Cyrus is irritated. Definitely. His way of speaking and the tone of voice tells me how pathetic I am.

Kinsey and Bryan came running after they saw me leaving the ground. I asked them to leave as both of them were involved in some events. Bryan had his shot-put match in a few minutes whereas Kinsey is in the disc throw.

I really regret stopping there. I have no idea why I stopped but something held me in place.

"Never mind" I said. "Never mind, never mind."

"But you do mind", said a small voice.

"No" I insisted.

For a while, it was quiet.

Then it said again, "you do."

And I replied, "I do, but it aches too much to admit."

I am *Pathetic*.

Compliments

Nice new stunning glimmer look
Fat feet ageing older foot
Shining standing staying strong
Crying carrying confident wrong
Praising praying all by heart
living Lying and falling apart
Happy charming changing hearts
Crashing breaking bruising at last

Chapter 26

Today is the last day of practice. The parade was going all good but, after we were told to merge with the boys, it is a complete mess.

The main problem is I am standing in the very front of the girls group. Whereas Bryan is standing at the very last from the boys' group because of his height. In short, he is standing right in front of me.

Whenever the parade is moving, his hands are hitting mine. Because of him, our whole group's movement is being disturbed. He accidentally hit my jaw once for which he had to listen for hours.

After a couple rounds, the coach decided to shift me and Kinsey in the front as he wanted two girls and two boys to hold the house flags.

We are now standing right in front of the three monkeys of our class. It feels like twisting the knife.

I am standing in front of Ethan and Cyrus; Kinsey is standing in front of Cyrus and Trevor. I hate this position already.

"Sir! People here are not aware of holding the flags properly I guess" here goes Ethan and his silly comments.

All three of them are the vice captains of their houses and instead of them, we got to hold the flags.

"I smell something burning." I mock. Still facing the front and not daring to turn back.

Ethan knew this was coming for him and he back fired.

"So do I... is someone feeling offended?" there he goes...

none of us are not talking to each other but the indirect comments were completely making sense.

"I was the vice-captain in my previous school. I know how to hold a flag right." I turned around and faced him while saying this.

"Sorry? Did I ask you something?" he said. Looking at Cyrus.

His 'sorry' is the most irritating part of him and the worst part is he knew I hated it.

"Did I say something to you?" I asked.

Kinsey burst into laughter and I had to turn to my position again otherwise I would have been starting civil war 2.

It's been an hour since we started today's practice and all the energy is drained out. Now that the seniors are back, the coach has gone crazy. Or I should say they have made the coach crazy. After a long fifteen-minute discussion, everyone decided that all the captains will be holding the flags.

'Wow... we are no longer required here' That's what my inner voice said to me. Now I have to deal with those girls again.

"The girls will be standing in the front. Olivia, you will be the first on the right side and Kinsey will be from the left." The coach said.

My lips curled into a smile then turned back to a flat line. Now that's more like it.

*****

Today is *the sports* day. All the students are given a white shirt with the school logo on it along with a white cap. The parade is about to start and one of the girls is feeling nauseous.

The chief guests have arrived and now that the fire has been lit to mark the beginning of the event, the parade starts.

Without any unnecessary mistake. It's done perfectly.

Once the Parade is done, it's time for the track events. I am cheering for my house, the red house.

Trevor was sitting on the stairs and I misunderstood him for someone else. I thought he is the one running in the 800-metre race.

"Come on Trevor!!!" I shouted so hard that most of the team members were looking at me. Including Trevor. I just want the earth to swallow me right now.

Though I am not sitting with my team, I am with Kinsey right now and she is not able to control her laugh at all. This is called a supportive friend acting like a jerk.

In the relay race, my house got second place. Bryan and his teammates tried a lot but they couldn't make it on time. I am waiting to congratulate Bryan but I couldn't see him around.

He is not in the field. Just in time I heard one of my juniors talking about Bryan. They are sitting right beside me so I could hear everything loud and clear.

"I saw him going out of the field to the badminton court area." The first kid is making it sound like a big deal.

"I know right! I saw the doctor looking for him." Said the other one.

Okay, this sounds like a big deal. After all its Bryan. He has a bad temper and when he has lost it, he could go far beyond his limits.

I don't have a good feeling about this. I turned to look at the medical counter and saw him standing with the doctor.

The look on his face says it all. Me and Kinsey ran towards him and all I could hear is everyone around whispering, all I could see was Bryan's Blood.

Chapter 27

Now that all the track events are done, it's time for the most interesting part. The tug of war. Boys are so excited about the event and so are girls. I am standing on the very front from my team and the captain is advising me how to pull the other team to our side.

"Grab the rope, pull it towards you and bend your body backwards" another senior of mine is asking me if I need spikes.

The match starts and everyone starts to shout.

"Come on Olivia!"

"You can do it."

"Bend backwards, pull the rope!"

These sentences are set on their tongues on repeat. Everyone around me is shouting like anything.

All I can hear is my name being shouted by each and everyone around me. I am about to fall but somehow, I managed to get the grip.

Linda is right behind me. She fell and she was well timed for the first time. We won the first match.

I got so energetic and the excitement is on another level.

The final match is between my house and Kinsey's house.

Eyes squinted; face wrinkled up. I am putting all my energy in it. That match felt like an actual competition but, my group is overpowering. I pulled harder. I could feel the rope in my control. I pulled more. They all falls down.

We ~~got~~ earned the first prize.

Bryan came to congratulate us but me and Kinsey are so angry with him that we ignored him all along. He punched his fist on the wall of the badminton court and his knuckles were torn and right hand covered in blood. Even after the stupid act, he was not going to the doctor as he thought they wouldn't allow him to participate in tug of war.

All my fingers are torn and my hands had so many band aids that they are looking like mummy's hands, thanks to the bloody rough rope. Kinsey fed me lunch and dinner. She is treating me like a baby who doesn't know how to use hands.

Linda is diagnosed with a fracture in the left leg. Bryan had three minor fractures in his hand. The day was very hectic and the more I stay here the more memories I created.

God knows how I ended up here of all places. There was no plan for me to go to a residential school. This all happened so fast that when I realised the fact that I am here for real, the year was about to end.

People say 'time runs.' I felt it for the first time and maybe, 'forever' is a word meant for memories, not people.

Speaking of which, the last event ~~for~~ with our seniors is coming up.

The farewell.

We were informed that farewell will be after ten days of the sports day.

*****

All of us headed towards the auditorium for the dance practice. The boys have decided to dance on some old funny songs for the farewell. A few minutes have passed and they have decided a few steps for the first song. The first step itself makes the dance funny.

All of them are going to jump like monkeys with a hand moment. Whenever they were doing this step me and Kinsey were howling with laughter.

It was naturally uncontrollable.

Chapter 28

The farewell is in the next two days.

I am sitting in the digital library, searching for small stage ideas. I just found an aesthetic sticky note small stage and before saving it, Trevor busts into the room. He is out of breath and looks like he climbed three floors at super speed.

"Go to city" he is looking at me but, I think he wanted to say this to the person behind me. I turn to look who he is referring to- there is no one behind me and he is still looking at me.

"Ethan is waiting for you in the admin" he is still saying it to my face.

"What? Who, me? WHY?" I am still not sure what he is talking about but, I am sure I heard him say city and admin.

"Fast!" he wipes the sweat off his face and looks at my screen.

"Is this for the small stage? It's great, now run to the admin. Get some better stuff" first he answers his question himself then asks me to get some stuff?

Without any further ado I decided to run to the admin because that's the only way to find out what are they up to. I can see Ethan and Cyrus standing together and they look puzzled. Before I could say anything, Ethan started to speak.

"They are not allowing you but, I want you to go even if I stay here." He says grabbing his head with both hands. His tone tells me he is worried.

Now... who are they? And why are they not allowing me to go? And where do I have to go? Trevor never conveys a proper message.

By looking at my face they both can tell I didn't understand a single word.

"We need decorative stuff for farewell, you and Ethan were supposed to go to the city. Management says they cannot allow two of you to go together. Ethan wants you to go if he is not allowed. But the management also doesn't want to send you alone. In simple words we might have to compromise with the stuff left after the commerce fest."

Cyrus explained everything to me in short and in the meantime, Ethan is called in the office. Before I could ask him anything else, Ethan called me to the office. The management head of the school is sitting in his glass cabin with a language teacher and both of them are firing questions on Ethan.

He gave them the list of required material and asked if only I could go. I am standing in the corner of the room, listening to their conversation. When they asked him why he wanted me to go?

He simply replied "because she knows the best when it comes to arts and creativity. And I wanted to go for the gifts we have to get for the seniors. But if you allow her and not me, I am fine with it and I can explain it to her."

wow... I mean, he is correct for the first time regarding my skills. The management head asks us to wait outside. Ethan then explains to me what the situation was and what it is going to be.

It is time for the juice break and the teacher asked us to have some juice and be back at the admin area. When I reached the admin area, I found out that we won't be going alone.

The teacher included four students from his class for their part of the farewell. All of them are our juniors and they were going to get the stuff for their small stage as grade 9th and 11th will be preparing two different stages for grade 10th and 12th.

We leave for the city market as soon as everyone go ready.

The first shop that we went to is very boring. They didn't have good options for the gifts. The options that we are liking are not available in bulk. Me and Ethan decided to stay quiet for the time being as we are given freedom to choose whatever we like.

Juniors spent two hours in the same shop and now everyone is hungry. We all wanted to take full advantage of being outside the school premises. I knew there is a famous sweet shop near this place and it is within walking distance.

I took a bunch of snacks for everyone but then Ethan warned me

"The teacher is going to pay for all of this from his personal money"

Without understanding his actual point, I replied foolishly "I'll ask the shopkeeper to call my father for the online payment"

"The teacher won't let you do that. He is responsible for whatever we do outside the premises and he won't involve parents in it." He whispered as we are standing close to the teacher.

That's when I realised what he is actually trying to say.

I feel embarrassed after acting without thinking about the consequences. I kept everything back in the place and the teacher saw it.

He asked why I kept them back but I simply said that no one likes those things. As it is a sweet shop, I could see all the attractive mouthwatering sweets on display.

Ethan went to one of the employees and asked if he could taste the sweets. I joined him in the process.

I hate sweets.

However, after eating the hostel food, everything is delicious for me. In the tasting session me and Ethan almost tried every sweet they had. Maybe we tried all of it.

More than thirty varieties just in one go. Right after we left the shop and Ethan closed the door behind us, we burst into laughter for what we did just now.

I never thought I'll be getting an experience like this. Especially in this year and with these people. The other shop that we went to is very small and I thought our work wouldn't be done in today's date.

While the teacher and his students are selecting rubber balloons, we purchased alphabetical balloons from here. Everyone is in this shop and the juniors are crowding this store.

"Let's go to that shop" I pointed at the shop next to this shop that also had decorating stuff. Ethan informed the teacher that he can find us in the other shop.

I went deeper into the shop and found some fancy paper fans. We are lucky to have it because they are the last pieces left. Karen followed us here to check if there is any useful thing for them.

When I am satisfied with the paper fans, I asked Karen to call the teacher to pay. She checked the other shop.

"No one is in there." She spoke.

"Just go and check in any other shop, they won't forget us" Ethan asked me to do so but I refused.

"You go and check, they are your classmates and your class teacher" Karen did as I asked her to.

In the meantime, me and Ethan checked our list of things. The paper fans aren't enough for the decoration.

Chapter 29

Karen never made it back.

"It's been ten minutes and she is not back." I started panicking. This street is completely unknown to all of us. What if–

"Stop overreacting. I will go and check what's the matter, till then stay here until I'm back." Ethan said just like he read my mind.

Now that Ethan is also gone, I have nothing to do but stare at the crowded street.

No sign of anyone. Ethan is gone from the past ten minutes. What am I going to do? What if I go somewhere and get lost? These thoughts kept me back for another five minutes but that's it. I cannot stay here a single minute anymore.

"You keep the stuff with you for now. My teacher or the boy who was with me will come to pay for this." I told the shopkeeper who was feeling bad for me as I got ditched.

Never thought this day would come. Me roaming around in the very unknown streets of this city. I just passed a small shop which has a very limited space for seating. More like a stall in concrete.

A white shirt with red horizontal stripes caught my eyes.

Ethan.

This roadside shop is five shops away from the gift store and I got a view of Ethan sitting inside the shop. When I looked around him, Karen is sitting with the teacher in front of him. Others are sitting beside him.

"Wow! And I thought you guys were lost!" The sound of my voice made everyone look at me and that's when I noticed the plates in their hands. Firstly, they ditched me and now they are enjoying the street food.

Great. How nice of them.

I somehow controlled my anger and jumped to the seat next to Theo. The tallest junior mostly misunderstood as a teacher by freshers. He offered me the dish but, I declined after looking at the condition of the shop.

Strong smell of frying oil which was being used for weeks now, dirty floor, suffocating sitting area, the fridge is so dirty that I would throw up anytime.

I took a bite from Karen's plate just to get the taste and decided not to risk my health. After the snack session, Ethan paid for that stuff from the cash given to him by the teacher and returned with a huge poly bag. The juniors also left their stuff there itself, Ethan had to get it.

The only thing remaining for our small stage are the sticky notes. Ethan called Mr. Aden and asked him about the gifts. We went to the shop suggested by Mr. Aden. Only me and Ethan got out of the van as the juniors are already done with their purchase.

There are a few stairs to the shop and it is bigger than the ones we visited before. It had a ton of options.

The gifts that we sorted out are so pretty and eye-catching. Ethan went to the teacher and asked him for the payment. Our figures are crossing the limit given by the school.

The teacher is ready to pay in cash but, he only had the money given by school which is not enough. He had enough money in his bank account but then the shopkeeper refused online transactions. It couldn't get any worst.

Ethan is hopping like a shuttlecock from the teacher to the shop. To save time both of us selected the stuff required in less than ten minutes but, this payment part took nearly an hour.

In the end, we had to leave all our fantasies there itself as the school strictly refused the payment. We went back to the first shop and Ethan gave the order for the stuff according to him.

Then while we are returning to school, we are discussing ice-cream.

"I hate chocolate. I mean I haven't had it in ages" Ethan explains his love for chocolate meanwhile the teacher asks the driver to stop the van on the opposite side of an ice-cream shop.

"I'll be back. Nobody will come out." the teacher orders us.

It's been 15 minutes and he is not back.

Another 20

Theo and Alex hop out of the van. I tried to stop them but, before I could argue they crossed the road and vanished in the shop.

Other 10 minutes

Ethan loses patience and jumps out.

"At Least come back and let us know what are they doing and how much time do we have to be trapped here." I try to say from the window.

I am in the backseat of the van with two little followers of the teacher and I have a thermocol sheet in my hand and my legs are trapped by the huge poly bags.

As soon as I asked Ethan, Seth started to shove the materials on me and Karen so that he could be free and join Ethan. I scolded him so badly that he cursed under his breath and finally sat quietly with a puffed-up face.

Another 10 minutes and I spotted a monkey eating ice-cream with full enjoyment. He vanished from the window when he saw me staring at him.

After a few more minutes, Ethan steps out of the shop. He has a cone in his hand. That rascal.

"Someone went to check on others" I gritted my teethes.

That monkey started laughing.

"Someone said they hate chocolate" I say staring at the chocolate cone in his hands.

Ethan is enjoying the chocolate ice-cream like he is getting to eat an ice-cream for the first and last time.

"I said I hate chocolate; this is *Belgian* chocolate." He smiled at me and continued to lick the flowing freaking ice-cream.

I hate him even more now.

*****

I am standing in the middle of the stage, holding one corner of the shiny wall hanging whereas Trevor is guiding me to fix it somehow to the wall.

This is the same wall hanging we used in commerce fest and kept it safe for this time. None of the newly purchased stuff has arrived and the time for the event is getting close.

Bryan starts to play some songs in the speakers connected to the computer in the assembly hall so that no one is bored. The juniors are blowing balloons for their small stage and Mateo brings a stapler to attach the black chart papers to our small stage.

Cyrus takes a stapler pin and pops one of their balloons. No one sees it though. Except me and Ezar. He has a mischievous smile on his face and he starts to pop more balloons. Ethan and Mateo join him in the process. Their goal is to destroy the balloons the juniors have already attached to their stage.

Unfortunately, one of the juniors catches them in the process and barks in front of everyone. No one is in a mood to spoil others' mood so; everyone went back to their work.

I am helping Ethan to attach the paper fans on the small stage and others are decorating the walls next to the small stage with a shiny lace. Both small stages are prepared in front of the main stage of the assembly hall, just some distance between them for the performances.

Only half an hour is left for the event to start and that's when our sticky notes arrived. Ethan and Trevor ran to the admin office to collect the stuff and when they reached the assembly hall, they started throwing one bundle in everyone's direction.

We were going to make a pattern with the sticky notes but now that it's already time, we somehow managed to make the small sage look decent by just pasting them randomly.

The seniors started to arrive and all of us are still in our morning clothes. Me and Kinsey ran towards our dormitory, changed into our party wear, styled our hair, and ran back towards the assembly hall.

I am wearing a pure silk cord-set that has dark red and black combination whereas, Kinsey is wearing a golden and creamy cord-set. We decided we would wear the same patten at every event.

It took us only ten minutes to get changed and be present here again. We wanted to do a little makeup but there is no sense in it as it would be washed away with our tears later tonight. I grabbed my packing papers on the way out as we will be needing it to pack the gifts.

Class 9th has already started their program and our whole class is sitting at the back stage, wrapping the gifts. There are stairs behind the main stage of the assembly hall from both the sides to go down the sports room. It is shaped like a 'V'

Each one of us is sitting on the stairs, some are cutting the packing sheets, some are cutting the tape and some are busy wrapping. Once we are done with the packing, it is already time for me to host the event for the senior most class.

I am shaking from head to toe and the thought of giving them 'farewell' is creeping in my head.

I am the host.

I am supposed to make the event memorable. I am expected to start this evening with lots of energy.

Yet, I messed up.

After starting the event horribly, all I could do was cry. I was supposed to give the best farewell to Grace. I stammered, I said the line I was not supposed to, and the worst part was I cried on the podium.

Once I am done with making the beautiful start a disaster, I went backstage, Trevor took the command and handled the rest of the event. The games planned for the seniors were refreshing, at least for them.

After everyone is done giving the gifts, our music teacher started singing a mashup. This is the most emotional part of the evening. All the seniors started crying. Boys left their seats and went out of the hall; girls are barely managing to keep their mascara in place.

I couldn't handle the pressure and when I went to check on others, backstage is all dark. The lamps are lit but its lights are not reaching here. It's already dusk.

I could hear someone sorbing. I went a little closer to check who it is. I stopped at the sight of the person. I am standing at the top of opposite stair case. I spot Kinsey holding someone's hand. Claiming them. I started running.

I fell down a couple of stairs.

My heart beats rushing.

I got up and again started to run.

My feet sore.

I stopped in front of Bryan and Cyrus.

My heart stopped.

Both are crying like babies. Adults but babies.

A tear fell on my hand and that's when I noticed they are not the only ones crying. Everyone around us is crying.

I am crying.

I never thought I would cry for some strangers or someone other than family. The realisation hit me directly in the heart, they are not strangers.

They are family.

Chapter 30

The few months I have spent here made those strangers a family. I never thought about it until now. The love, hatred, happiness, disappointments, memories full of fun, bad times, all this we shared in these few months made us more than strangers.

My seniors were always with me. They supported me a lot. They guided me throughout the year. They treated me like their younger sister. They treated me like their own family member.

This event, the fuss, the crying sessions, the hard work, was all worth it. This was the least we could do for them.

Once everything is over, all the seniors are called on the stage. Each one of them is crying. Sobbing. Hugging each other.

I cried so much tonight that my face is matching my red outfit and my black robe is highlighting it.

There is red carpet on the floor of the dining hall leading the seniors to their seats. Dining hall is giving the farewell vibe with the pink and blue lights. All the plates are already arranged for us on the tables.

After we are done with dinner, everyone went back to their dorms. I am about to change my clothes and someone knocked on the door.

Blair asked us to get back into the outfit.

Once we are done, all of them asked us to sit in the centre of the room. All five of them surrounded us. They are standing. We are on our knees.

A ton of thoughts running through my mind right now.

I have no idea what is going on here. Are they gonna hit us? Or what are they going to do?

Both of us closed our eyes and suddenly something fell on us.

Someone fell on us.

Me and Kinsey opened our eyes.

All of them hugged us.

They acted like they were about to slap us but, they hugged us.

I am expressionless. What just happened shocked me from head to toe. I let out a shaky laugh. Everyone started laughing. The difference is that everyone is laughing with the tears pouring out from their eyes. All of us are crying.

Again.

We are sitting in a circle on the floor. Holding onto each other tightly. Not wanting to let go. This is the last event we got to enjoy together. The very last for *everyone in this room*. I get goosebumps all over my body on this thought.

After a proper thirty-minute crying session, everyone went to their rooms. I have shared so many memories with them that the thought of spending them without them irritates me the most. Now that everyone is gone, Kinsey is half asleep, my mind won't shut down.

I wonder who will explain the works to the newcomers as they will have no seniors. I had my seniors to guide me to the ways but they won't have us. Who will make them experience new fun ways to things.

How to tackle the events and especially the farewell. Moreover, who are the girls going to give the farewell to? I feel bad for them even if I don't know them. Who is going to guide them to hide the truck? feels awful.

Still, I don't have any other option.

They are going to miss all the fun parts in the hostel. The funny moments of Sunday or the experience of having seniors. They will have no one to share their happy memories or the saddest ones.

Grace ~~was~~ is that senior for me. I shared every single detail of my life with her which felt like sharing things with an elder sister. I don't think I would have been a senior like her but I would have enjoyed that role. Now that all of them are going to part their ways I feel bad as well as happy.

I feel happy for them that they will be pursuing their dreams and preparing harder to achieve it but, as I got less than a year to spend time with them, I feel bad that we would have made a lot more memories only if I had come sooner.

Wearing their decent clothes for some industrial visits or borrowing traditional stuff for any occasion was another level of fun.

I can't remember a single time when Blair was the only one wearing her clothes during the movie nights. Half of her wardrobe was always distributed among the juniors.

Tonight is the first time I cried so much for someone.

Wish I could just stop the time or just press a rewind button to enjoy all these moments once again to the fullest. Someone once said, "if something makes you feel sad, it must have been pretty wonderful when it was happening." This chapter of my life is one of the most marvellous of all.

*****

Days are going well. I started going to basketball again. Ezar, Bryan, and Rufus wait for me and Kinsey near the dining hall to go for Basketball together.

As Trevor always goes for table tennis, Bryan brings his Basketball to play. He is the only one who had his personal basketball but, today Trevor is playing Basketball with his group and the sports room is locked.

We wanted to play so bad that we broke in.

Me and Kinsey weren't involved directly in it. It was all Bryan's idea. He opened the screw of the window and gave it to Rufus. He jumped inside and when he was searching for the basketball Rufus threw that screw away.

The sports room was completely dark and Bryan was not visible to us. When Bryan jumped out with the ball in his hand, he started cursing Rufus as they needed the screw to close the window back.

Whereas me and Kinsey couldn't control our laughs and the fear of getting caught in the middle of robbery was flying over our heads.

We were basically robbing the school property but, as it was in the premises only, we considered it borrowing. We saw a security guard was heading in our way and all of us started acting like we were here to drink water.

There were two water coolers just in front of the sports room. Bryan and Rufus drank some water from there and came back to us as we stood in the middle of the walkway. Bryan is acting cool and flexing the ball in his hand.

"Did you know my father sent this ball through courier?" he looked at me like it really is true.

He is such a manipulator.

"Are we not going to keep it back in the place after we are done?" I asked just to be sure.

They are keeping it back, right? The thought strikes my mind that if they were going to return it, they wouldn't have made these efforts.

"Return to whom? It's mine. Just now I told you my father got it." He winked. This freaking manipulator is going to get us in trouble. Ezar missed all the fun part today.

When we are heading towards our hostels, Bryan saw the principal heading in our direction. We are standing in front of the IT lab. The boys' hostel and girls' hostel are separated from here. It is already time for the study prep, it's compulsory for boys to go to their respective classes and girls are to be present in the hostel.

We. are. late.

Principal is on round to check on the boys. It is acceptable if girls are late one or two times. For boys, he won't tolerate it. Bryan shoved the stolen object in my hand and both of them started to run for the class.

What am I supposed to do with it?

Now I have to give a proper explanation where I got this freaking basketball from.

Great!

Chapter 31

Today is 'Punch Day'.

After the assembly, everyone was punching each other in front of our class. Kinsey went and punched Ethan. Her hand barely touching his tricep. His expression is unreadable. He crossed his arms on his chest and shouted.

"Everyone come here! Get a punch from her."

She was so embarrassed by his comment as his playful tone made everyone laugh, including her. I am quiet. I touched no one.

Cyrus and Kinsey were already fighting over something and he stapled her bag. She got furious and did the same in return. I supported Kinsey and that idiot stapled my water bottle. After a while, he started throwing broken pieces of a calculator at me.

I am used to him shooting paper balls at my head as it is a routine in economics class but *calculator* keys?

I took the opportunity and punched him at the back with my full force. I am always late at realising things and after doing anything, I regret it. Just like now.

Why did I hit him? devils!

He is the only one in the class who can hit anyone without a single sight of hesitation. I'm doomed.

We did complete five rounds of the class as he is trying to hit me and I am running like a duck. Unfortunately, it is a free class so no teacher is expected in the class for the next forty minutes.

Kinsey and Bryan are sitting out of the class, on the stairs. When I am at the door, facing Cyrus. Bryan called me out. I walked backward, still facing Cyrus. Bryan asked me to sit. I didn't.

How will I? Knowing that death is surrounding me.

"Sit down, he won't do anything" Bryan asked once again in a more serious tone. I sat.

Just when I was about to touch the floor, he punched me.

That bloody rascal. I didn't hit him *that* hard. It felt like my backbone would come out from my chest. Well, that's a bit of exaggeration but still, it is painful.

"Are you crazy?! You psycho bastard! She is a girl! How can you hit her so hard?! Go to the class. Right now!" he yelled. Anger exploding in him. Now Bryan is shouting like a psycho bastard. He just exaggerated everything.

Meanwhile as Cyrus is already in a fun mood, he pissed Bryan more by saying "Aww... it's okay. She isn't dead, is she?"

Bryan is already in the worst mood today. He is ordering everyone around and showing that we did something to upset him. Whatever, who cares?

Today I am wearing a black and white Chex shirt. I think at least a thousand times before wearing this as the whole school has it and I do not want to twin with anyone.

As always out of luck, every other kid who has it been wearing it. I am sitting in my place back in class and out of nowhere someone starts to laugh. Then the laughter is continued by the person next to him.

Trevor says, "what are you studying? You know you are not scoring much more than the topper..." he laughs at others.

Topper who?

"The real topper is here, silent killer..." he is now saying this in such a way that makes me want to understand the reason behind the whole story.

That's when I realised, he is talking about me. I scored the highest marks in economics in the first-class test.

Why now? Do they really enjoy mocking every other person all the time?

I am holding the economics reference book... OH...

I was so into deep thoughts about what will be in dinner tonight, I didn't realise which book I am holding. Now they think I am focused. Technically I am but, not about anything else other than food.

*****

Dear Dairy,

I have no idea what time and date it is. What I know is I keep forgetting to mention crazy stuff to you.

It's been two days since Kinsey is gone. She had some tissue injury on her left hand and the school allowed her leave for a week.

Yesterday was Friday. The day every student is afraid of. The day I enjoy the most. The day to test one's public speaking skills. I had a feeling that I will be called. The topic was displayed on the main screen in the assembly hall at the last moment and random names are called out to share their thoughts.

Last Friday, Bryan was there with the person who was supposed to take the names. I already asked him to let me know in advance. He gave me the signal which said my name was there.

The topic was very random. 'Health is wealth'.

The announcer notices that I have been warned, he skipped my name. I was sure if my name was skipped, it will be their next time for sure. It was also our English activity yesterday.

We were supposed to prepare a speech on any topic of our choice. My topic was "trust."

I have experienced a ton of types of trusts this year. I decided this would be a perfect topic to keep my thoughts on. Last time when this activity happened, I spoke on the famous saying "honesty is the best policy."

The English activity took place in the auditorium.

Trevor hosted the activity and he introduced everyone. All of us shared our thoughts on very different topics and tried to match it with current affairs. Exams were getting close and everyone started to focus more on the academic part.

As I was not called on the stage last Friday, there was a 101 percent chance me being called yesterday. When the topic for the day was displayed on the screen in the assembly hall, I was the first person called on the stage. The topic was still interesting.

"A house is not a home."

There was so much I could speak on this. Later that day, our class with the 9th graders were taken for a company visit. A milk factory.

When we reached there, we were asked to wait as the person who was supposed to be with us was running late. I was the only senior from the girls' side as Kinsey is not there.

All of us were sitting on the lawn. It's small. All the boys are sitting in a corner while all the girls are sitting in the centre. One of the girls stands up and suggests playing something. I joined her. Every girl joins her. The boys looked uninterested so no one bothered to ask them. We started with the knock-knock game and went till ice and water.

When all of us exhausted ourselves, that person arrived. He gave a brief about the factory before entering the unit. Then the first thing I saw was the packaging part. The milk was being packed in different polybags at different quantities.

Then as we moved further, there was a huge container kept in a room. He explained to us the whole process of milk Pasteurisation. As we moved further, the smell of milk was everywhere in the surrounding area. After we reached the end, all of us got a pack of sweetened yogurt.

Chapter 32

Kinsey is back and now she is as good as she could be. Her hand is healed and exams are close. Last night we were not able to sleep and as for studies we were done for the day. So, we sneaked into one of our juniors' rooms.

Seniors are not allowed to go downstairs after 10 P.M.

We crawled on the floor so that their house parent wouldn't spot us from the window. Unfortunately, the room we wanted to go into was just beside the house parents' room. This junior is also known for singing. Her vocals are super good. The room was dark. Her roommates were sleeping.

Me and Kinsey started with some horror stories for entertainment.

It was half past midnight when we were discussing a lady with white clothes just like any other basic ghost. A security guard was walking outside the hostel and she was visible from the window on the back. One of the girls freaked out when she was half asleep and listening to us.

Just then some knocked on the door.

A piece of white cloth was visible to all of us from the main window. The door opened.

No voice.

No sign of life.

The door opened a little more. It creaked.

Everyone started to freak out except me.

I knew what was happening.

I tried to hide.

Kinsey got my signal and she tried to cover herself.

The girls started to tremble.

They started to hide themselves.

I hit one of the girls on the head and whispered "why the hell are you hiding? We are not supposed to be here. If you are found missing from the room, you are dead."

she freaked out more. "Dead? What do you mean?"

I wanted to laugh out loud but due to the situation I controlled myself somehow. She is still in the horror story rather than noticing her house parent is standing on the door and checking on everyone. Not to mention the white clothes.

"Who is here?" from the voice of the house parent, the girls jumped on their feet.

"It's us, we were just going to sleep" she said acting innocent. my my... how polite.

"I think I heard someone talking." I could feel the seriousness in her voice.

"Oh yes, we were just going through the day." That little liar added.

"Sleep right now or I will not let you in my class tomorrow." This lady really knows how to make them follow the schedule. She started to leave but before I could hear her walk out, her footsteps stopped.

"And It would be good for you to go to your room" she added.

"But isn't this our room?" The girls are still playing fool.

"Oh, I was talking to Olivia and Kinsey" she smiled and left the door open on her way out.

Makes sense. I was in the laundry basket and Kinsey was behind the curtains. Not to mention the almost see through laundry basket is never full at night and the curtains are of her knee length.

*****

Today is National Science Day as well as our little future scientists' birthday, Denise. She has not been attending classes for a while now but today she showed up. The assembly hall is completely packed with stalls. I helped my classmates this morning in setting their stall.

Each one of them had prepared a different project. Bryan made a Hologram 3D projector. Whereas, Ezar prepared the project based on electrostatic energy and Jay made a Tesla coil.

Other than this, the juniors also prepared amazing projects with their super cool presentations. All the city locals are allowed to visit the exhibition. I somehow managed to inform my mom yesterday. I have a relative living nearby. I asked mom to inform them so that they could bring me some snacks.

Unfortunately, none of the commerce department members are allowed in there. I am sitting outside of my class, studying business studies. The class is giving the lazy vibes so I brought my desk with me. I am sitting in front of the door, touching the pillar in the porch. Cyrus always likes this spot but, since he is in the class I am already sitting here.

Speak of the devil.

Cyrus glares at me and asks me to move. I am stubborn. I didn't move. He started to push me with a notebook. I pushed back. He moves to the side of my desk and picks it up. The table and the chair are joint. I start to slide and end up on the floor.

I glared back at his laughing face and stomped inside the class. He thinks he is the only one who can win, that's where he is wrong.

I am back again but, this time with another desk. His desk. I settled on the other side of the door. He is watching me wide eyed but he chooses to remain silent. I appreciate it though.

Both of us discussed some topics and now I feel sleepy. I put my head down and try to take a nap. Someone is whispering something in my ear a few minutes later.

The voice feels familiar but I am not able to understand a single word. The words are not making sense. I opened my eyes and I was no longer in the city of dreams, murdering every single person I hate. Cyrus was not in his place and someone with a familiar tone spoke something again. Something I should be knowing and I should be excited for. Then realisation hits.

"Your relatives are here" Bryan whispered for the third time and I jumped in my seat. He was bent on his knees and whispering in a very low voice as to avoid getting caught.

I looked around to check what he was hiding from and found nothing. I stare blankly at him. He rubs his forehead and says, "I am not allowed to leave the stall and you are not allowed to come there, your teacher is busy with others inside the class. Hurry up and come once I leave. If he sees you going that side, he won't let you sit here, so come fast and don't get caught." He stands up and cleans his trousers on the knees.

Oh yes! I was supposed to be there at this time. I give him assurance that I am back to me and I will be there in a while. He leaves as soon as I am up. Cyrus appears from the door and asks me if he is gone.

"How did you know he was here?" Didn't he say he was not to be caught? I ask him, still half asleep.

"He asked me to distract the teacher" he replied dryly.

Fine that way. I ran towards the assembly hall and made some efforts to not get caught. I could spot my uncle standing in the corner. When I reached him, he called my aunt and my cousin who were convincing the management head for permission to meet me.

They are having two chocolates and two boxes of my favourite chips. This is when the problem arises. I do not have a backpack and the stuff is not small enough to fit in my pockets. I don't even have pockets in these pants.

Great.

I asked my cousin to call Bryan. But how do they know each other. Before I could ask this any of them, my cousin spoke

"He was the only one who looked a bit older as compared to the rest of the people, I asked him if he knew you and he told me to wait so that he can call you. Simple." His description was enough for me to understand the connection.

Bryan comes with his bag; I shove all the stuff inside it and he acts like he is heading for the class in front of all the other people while crossing the front part of assembly hall. Thankfully because of the stalls, outside of the assembly hall is not visible. Bryan entered from the back side again. I called mom from my aunts' cell phone and informed her that I am doing well. I went back to my class where Cyrus was already waiting for me.

"Where is my chocolate?" he asked me, I guess...

"YOUR chocolate?" I asked him in a very politely terrifying way.

"You don't want to solve your doubts, do you?" he grins.

shoot! I completely forgot he was going to teach me business studies and this jerk won't do it for free.

"All the things are in Bryan's bag; he will hand them to me later." I speak.

"Later when?" he raised one eye brow.

"Okay! Just solve my doubts and I'm going to get the stuff myself!" I say irritatingly. The exam is next week and this jerk could fight all year. He smirks. I can tell he doesn't believe me by the look on his face.

"Let's go and get done with it, then we will continue with this" he picks my book from the table and goes to the teacher in the class. He takes permission saying that we must talk to Mr. Joe urgently.

We are finally behind Bryan's stall but all the ways from the back side are blocked. I whispered Ezar's name from the curtains as I thought he is standing just right on the other side.

He asked us to wait. I could spot a few teachers roaming around and I thought it better to hurry. Then out of nowhere Bryan suddenly came to us and he handed me a chocolate. The biggest one. Cyrus somehow managed to shove it inside his pocket.

After we went back to the class, he gave the chocolate to me only to snatch it again and gulped more than half of it. I swear on his life that I will never ever forget that.

Business studies aside, when Bryan gave me my stuff, I went to my hostel and kept my bag in my wardrobe. I ran back towards the assembly hall. I met with Ezar's and Jay's parents and talked to my mom once again and I am finally feeling free.

Soon after all the fun, exams are getting close. I got busy studying. Everyone is busy studying. Due to studying till late at night, everyone in the class is completing the sleep in Economics class. The teacher keeps on teaching to himself and all of us take a good nap. I have never slept in a class my entire life but, in this class, especially with this teacher in front of me, my eyes and my brain forcefully shut down every time in this class.

Chapter 33

I am standing in front of Mr. Brandon and waiting for him to give me a movie. We decided to play the guessing game as no one is in a mood to study.

Mr. Brandon wrote a movie on the newspaper lying in front of him on the table and I am supposed to act on it so that my team mates get to guess it.

I am acting for the word "young" so that all of my classmates can guess something related and their wild guesses were literally on rapid fire.

"Child"

"kid"

"cute"

"kind"

"beautiful"

"Little baby"

"smile"

"fair"

"ugly" Ethan snapped. Then he laughed.

wait what? I am simply keeping my index finger on my cheek and smiling like a kid so that they can guess something related to young but, ugly?

Ethan's guesses are always ugly.

Another minute and Trevor got the movie correct.

Mr. Brandon is giving completely unknown movies to us and by luck some of us are able to guess some.

*****

Exams are going on rapid fire, there is no time to study everything but we are trying to cover as much as we could. I have my economics exams tomorrow and as no one is there in the class, I decided to sit on the stairs outside. Ethan, Trevor, and Cyrus went to the library and the science students are sitting in the gazebo which is in the opposite lawn of our class, beyond the pond.

I can see all three of them focused on the study material from the spot I am sitting. Kinsey, Henry, and Mateo are sleeping in the class and before I could sleep, I came out.

I have completed two chapters since I came and now, I need a break. Otherwise, I am going to forget everything all together.

I am lost in my own thoughts just when Kinsey comes out of the class and leans on the pillar exactly opposite to me. She also brought her stuff to study. We don't talk for another hour and that's when a voice catches our attention.

"So, you are gonna top huh?" sounds like Mateo

"Shut your ******* mouth" and this sounds like Mateo just triggered Henry. Both of them are shouting so loud that my ear drums might get damaged.

"Shut up both of you! We are trying to study here can't you see?" I yelled from outside.

Mateo showed me thumbs up from the window.

"No, we won't stay quiet" Henry barked. And he pissed me off.

Getting pissed off by something said by him was the very last thing on my mind right now but he just did what he shouldn't have done. He started to shout in double volume. This time he is cursing a little too much than he should.

All I could think was go and punch him in the face but I can see the principal walking in our direction.

Perfect timing sir. I approached his as he reached near our class.

"Hello sir, we are trying to study but the people in our class are cursing loudly and when I asked to stop politely, they won't understand. Mateo is good but Henry is the main problem." I blurted out. The principal stomped inside the class and gave them a good speech.

Now that everything is quiet again, I start to study.

*****

Today's economics exam was horrible. Even after studying in the corridor for almost an hour, I was able to stuff my head with some definitions and nothing else.

Kinsey was sitting on the floor, at the back side of our class. Me and Ethan were walking in a circle around the porch between our class and the science section, Cyrus was on his usual spot with Henry and Mateo. Jay, Bryan, and Ezar were in their own depression zone.

This morning, Kinsey and I took our economics book with us during the physical training and unfortunately Ethan, Trevor and Cyrus saw us. They made fun of us as we were lost in the book at 6 freaking A.M.

I have set an alarm for 4 A.M.

Again.

Tomorrow is the second last exam, business studies. I have planned my study schedule and if I start at 4, I will be able to complete everything by 6. I will go through the main parts before going to the examination hall. As business studies is not as vast as economics, I think I'll be able to complete it on time.

I woke up to my alarm at 4. Me and Kinsey made our favourite snack which is macaroni. Kinsey is sitting at her usual spot which is her bed. She prefers to sit on her bed or the study table for studying whereas, I like to sit on the balcony of our dormitory.

That is the only spot where the fresh air is passing through and the path outside the dormitory to the dining hall is visible. The air currently is a little cold and I am sitting in my favourite blue shorts, my white mickey mouse T-shirt which is covered with my puffer jacket.

I made myself a cup of black coffee to keep me awake and as soon as I spilled the coffee on my T-shirt, I kept the cup aside and ignoring the mess I started to study.

After a while, I am feeling dizzy, I guess I will just take a 15-minute nap and complete everything.

The exam is going to start in the next 30 minutes and here I am standing with my two duplicates fighting for the clothes 'who was supposed to wear black today.'

Firstly, I ate macaroni and drank black coffee at 4 A.M. for god's sake and slept.

Secondly, I have no idea what I am going to write in the exam.

And lastly, I am looking like Trevor and Bryan for hell's sake or I should say they are looking like me. I decided to wear black shirt 2 days ago and here they are, both of them in black shirts, what a coincidence. Luckily, Trevor is wearing beige pants whereas Bryan is wearing grey ones.

This morning, I asked Kinsey for my beige pants and she suggested that I wear grey but I finally wore green. So, it makes me different. Thank God!

I am sitting at my favourite spot which is the platform next to the stairs of our class. Here is a white vase kept upside down. Which makes a good stool. Cyrus is sitting on that vase beside me and he is basically teaching me. Explaining important points.

Chapter 34

Today was the last exam. After the exam, when Kinsey was done begging Ethan, Trevor, and Cyrus to write a letter for me, everyone left for snacks. I told her that I am going to leave tomorrow on my birthday and won't be coming back.

Means these were my last days with the best friend group I ever had. I requested from Kinsey that I want a handwritten letter from everyone on my birthday. I made sure when she asked them it must look like she wants them to write it for me, without me knowing.

She has been asking them for a month and they won't listen but, after today's exam they said they will give it to me tomorrow and according to my calculations tomorrow is going to be a really very hard day for god's sake.

3 hours passed, and Ezar and I were still throwing water at each other. As the finals are done, none of us is having any work to keep us occupied.

We thought that going back to the hostel would be a waste of our time and boring too. When I was talking to Kinsey in front of our class, Bryan was standing next to me. He and Ezar were throwing water at each other. Ezar was aiming for Bryan but Bryan jumped out of the way and now the water is dripping down my sleeve.

I ran towards Ezar in the lawn and this tom and jerry show went on for a good 15 minutes. "Let's meet at sports" I said to them as it will be my last time there.

Me and Kinsey are wearing the same sports pants, we walk down the slope of the badminton court and I can see some people playing inside. Everyone in the campus is busy studying for the exams so all the sports areas were empty and some people in the badminton court are none other than my fellow classmates.

The indoor court has three courts in it. I spot Ethan v/s Trevor, Mateo v/s Henry and Cyrus v/s Jay. Basketball court is a few blocks away from here. Its an outdoor court. Actually two outdoor courts beside the skating ring and in front of the lawn tennis court.

Me, Kinsey, Rufus, Ezar and Bryan chatted a little and now I am back in front of the dining hall after the sports time ended and Bryan left for his home. Kinsey returned to the hostel but I am going to the IT lab for a bit. I am sitting with Jay and we are discussing an anime.

Just then Ethan and Cyrus enter the room. Ethan called me to the computer he is using and his face looks like a puppy who is about to demand something. Something which *can* be fulfilled.

The IT lab is a long room with 8 tables. Each table has five systems but the last 2 rows are allotted to the seniors. That includes us.

"You are going home tomorrow, right? Ethan asked me as he pulled his chair closer to the table.

"Yes, but wh-" before I could finish, he cuts me off

"So that means your parents are coming...... Which means they will be standing on the main gate..." He pauses. Looks at me.

I know what he is going to say next but I ask anyway

"Get to the point, what are you trying to say?"

"I have a list of things I want and I have a plan to get them." He says in excitement.

I laugh, I just laugh like a maniac. Firstly 'The Ethan' is asking 'me' for a favour and secondly, he wants my parents to sneak in his stuff which is food for sure. He is always hungry for packaged food and food other than whatever healthy food is prepared for us in here.

"And what makes you think that I will ask my parents for it?" I ask. His lips curl into a thin smile and I know this look. He thinks that he will be able to convince me this time too and this time, he is wrong.

"Don't you think you should make yourself useful before going? at least for once? And if you want me to starve myself it's okay. I will have another opportunity" he says *'for once'* huh...

"Who said I am *not* going to help you?" I speak. He smiles again with hope in his eyes

"But I am not going to help you, you must help yourself. You have my mother's mail ID, right?" I grin. he stops smiling.

He is blank for a second and the fact that he must mail my mom from his side hits him.

Randomly, Unexpectedly, he opens my mom's mail and types the list. Crosschecking with Cyrus for all the necessities. That list is a bit too long and he feels it too. He removed some items even when I asked not to.

Then he asks me to cross check and hits the send button.

*****

It's already 11 P.M.

I have been kicked out of my room with the fiction novel I am reading from past a week. I am told to sit somewhere far from my room so that it is not visible to me.

I am sitting on the stairs in front of the water cooler. The moon is bright and calm tonight. The stars are shining, a cold breeze gives me goosebumps, moonlight on my face, the darkness in the passage and the silence in the hostel.

During this time usually the hostel is always full of laughs. Some people sit down stairs with their groups, some are always playing some childish games and some are always busy with their work.

Tonight, the hostel feels so quiet that the silence is screaming in my head. I can hear the water cooler fill, footsteps downstairs even when I am sitting in the last corner of the building. Then I remember that everyone is busy studying for their next exam.

Memories of my past strikes me. When I first came and how I felt. Then I made friends. Then teachers started to appreciate me. How I used to get sick in every 2 months. From setting my schedule, getting used to the routine, to enjoying the place I first thought was another version of jail.

I remember all the events all of us used to organise together, those movie nights, the cricket matches, those times when all of us used to plan and bunk the classes, how we used to get on our teachers nerves, how I was to blame for anything which went wrong even though it might not be my fault, how my classmates used to taunt me in everything then come begging for their work to be done and lastly how all of us spent a great time together.

I never thought I would find such a group, these people, and the memories with them were my best times and I'd love to cherish these memories for the rest of my life.

This group of idiots made me fall in love with the place. When I was a fresher, no one tried to approach me and I didn't even know their names after spending a month but, when we started to work together, be it in the class or on the stage, we have gotten much closer than I thought.

Before I could think of anything else, I realised that my hands are wet. There are droplets on the back of my hands and when I try to look up to check whether it's raining, reality hits me hard. It's not the rain.

It's me.

I have no idea when I burst into tears.

Damn me.

It's 12:00 A.M. sharp.

"Happy seventeen to me" I whispered to myself.

Kinsey, Grace and one of my favourite junior Eden. All three of them pop out from the corner and hug me tightly. They wish me well.

"Really sorry babe. You must wait a little longer before you come into the room. We are not done yet." Kinsey apologises to me.

She seems excited as well as upset. Maybe because both of us know this will be our last night together and we have no idea when we will get to see each other once I leave.

I nod and smile back as I am not in a condition to speak anything and they disappeared in the dark again.

Kinsey did a ton of mistakes since she came. We fought every time but, she changed. Before forgiving her every time I used to ask myself if it's the right thing to do.

I was the only one for her and she was the only one for me. We were together 24/7 from past 8 months. How would have we survived otherwise. When I think of that now, I feel happy for what I did.

Not wanting me to be left alone, especially at this moment, they came back after 15 minutes and took me to the room. As I enter my room, it's completely dark.

Then I noticed the fairy lights on my bookshelf.

My compartment is the last one in the room. It has the best view and there is a different peaceful vibe in that corner. I just can't stop bragging about it now.

As I am walking closer, I can see balloons all over my bed, the side wall, and my study table.

I gasp as soon as my eyes land on my wardrobe… There is a white "Birthday Girl" sash attached to the door for me to take it out and wear it, the most awesome part is my wardrobe doors are filled with handwritten notes.

Words just can't express what I am feeling right now. I notice that those balloons on the wall are not empty, Kinsey wrote every tagline and every nickname I was given by my friends.

Kinsey gifted me a silver bracelet, Grace and Eden simply made the arrangement for the decorative stuff and I have no idea how they managed to get me the biggest chocolate.

None of this feels real, these people I never knew existed a few months ago or they never knew I existed, still made me feel super *happy*. They are ~~like~~ a family to me now. Grace and Eden left early as both of them had a ton of work, still they managed to take some time for me and I really really appreciate that.

    It's me and Kinsey

    Kinsey and me

    We hug each other

    and I cried the shit out of me.

Fantasy

Sitting like a statue, they are lost
Lost in thoughts, all they want
Wanting to be lost forever
The sweet loving hope of crazy terrifying adventures
From fighting dragons to being the ruler of the world
Being a Princess to strange wizard
Casting spells and whooshing wands
Feeding Pokémons and mowing lawns
We all have our own kind of world
"Only if it was real"
Slapping on the face facing reality
Back to the place we are meant to be
Fantasising in "dreams"
We die every night only in the hope of waking on the other side
That side changes every night
And that's how we live fantastically thousand lives

Chapter 35

The sun is shining bright, my face is on another level of glow. Credit goes to the breakdown last night. I stand up from my bed and see myself in the mirror. I have got puffy eyes and the credit goes to the same.

I jump around Kinsey and snatch her blanket away. It's been 2 months since we are sleeping together on the floor. We drag our mattress down every night and sleep together.

She is used to my annoying tricks to wake her but today surprisingly she woke up just after I snatched her blanket and shouted that this day is supposed to be my best day. In my sixteen years of life, I never ever imagined I'd be starting my seventeenth chapter here. My first birthday ever when my parents weren't there to wish me at night. Just like we did for Jane, my friends did the best for me.

I changed into my favourite lavender shirt with black trousers. I kept it preserved for this day. As we leave the hostel for breakfast, everyone on the way to the dining hall is wishing me. The day feels nice. I feel like I am free, free, free...

We are standing in front of the dining hall and everyone is leaving for classes. Now the whole space is empty. Me and my classmates, all of us are waiting for the bus. We are going to a museum as a field trip. The place is located right in front of our school as it is also the school's property.

A bunch of juniors' rush towards me to give me some personalised hand written notes, some brought flowers from God knows where, some made me cute keychains.

Rose pops up in front of me from pushing the crowed away.

"I am going to read the news today and I will announce your name." she says with a mischievous smile on her face.

I ~~am~~ *was* one of the news readers in the assembly and today it *was* my turn. The news reader announces the birthday of the day for a small assembly celebration. I had a bet with her that my name won't be announced. It's too embarrassing to stand idle in the middle of the crowed.

"You are going to read the news but even willingly you won't be able to take my name." I said with a sweet smile.

"Why?" she asked completely confused.

I pointed towards the bus waiting for us in the corner.

"We are going on a field trip" I grinned and added "*before* assembly."

"Oh NO! That's not fair!" she covered her face with the new paper in her hand showing me a glimpse of new headlines and ran back towards the assembly hall as she is already ten minutes late.

As soon as we reach there, we are asked to wait for some time. Before directly going to the museum, we are in a place which is surrounded by flowers and grass. The platform I am standing on is made of stones and has beautiful flowers hanging from the roof.

We did a photo session while waiting. Then some people came with a wooden case in their hands. Each one of them has their own. Now that they are here, we start with an exercise and then all of us sit on the floor. The people open their cases and there is a hand loom in each one.

We got to learn the weaving process and it was enjoyable. After weaving, we were called by our teacher who brought us here. He took us to the museum. The guide to the museum gave each one of us a small cell phone connected with the earphones so that wherever we are going, the explanation will be played.

The two-hour museum tour was mind-blowingly fantastic. In my opinion everyone should visit that place for once.

When we were taken back to the school, I literally begged everyone to play something as I knew it is my *last* day.

No one is listening to me and now I am furious. I went straight to the dining hall for lunch. Kinsey and Ethan are calling me outside to play but, I have made up my mind that I won't listen to them a bit.

Kinsey tried to convince me so much but I know that a dog's tail can never be straight. Ethan is just doing everything for formality as he just wants the sweets.

Our campus allows students to celebrate their birthdays by distributing sweets. The sweets are ordered according to the number of teachers and classmates the birthday person has.

I have ordered one small and two large boxes of the sweets which are probably lying in the post box at the admin area.

I go directly to the hostel to change my shirt because I don't want to ruin it before clicking pictures tonight at home. I changed into a comfy reddish t-shirt and headed towards the admin office.

When I was crossing my class I could hear Ethan, Kinsey, Cyrus, and others shouting my name.

"Come back, Olivia!" Ethan started first.

"Let's play something!" He continued.

"We are sorry!" someone yelled and I left.

Ignoring all of them while going to the admin office, I took a stop in my seniors' class as it is just beside the office. Grace hugged me, my house captain waved me good luck, and others wished me the best. Now that I have my sweets, I distributed it to every teacher I saw on my way to class.

As soon as I enter my class. Ethan is sitting on my table with Cyrus next to him. Kinsey is standing close to the door and Trevor is standing beside her.

"Here is your box. Bye." I shoved a large box of sweets in Ethan's hand and turned around to leave.

"Oi! Who wants the sweets? We are here for you. We wanted to play something together. Right boys?" Ethan cleared his throat, giving a sign to everyone that they should start convincing me.

"But I don't want to play with people who are just selfish and doing this because they owe me." I have my back facing them to ignore their faces and tried my best to sound disappointed and rude even though I am the only one who is badly interested in playing.

Everyone blocked my way out. Kinsey is controlling her laugh. Ethan is throwing words at me which doesn't make any sense just because he is the one saying them.

"Move" I said to Cyrus who is guarding the door like they have kept an endangered species. He won't shift an inch.

"Move" I hissed. Jay refused.

This is getting interesting and I know they won't move. I still tried to leave but still no one would listen.

"Let's play goal-spot" I finally decided. Everyone suddenly started to run and make the circle before I got a chance to change my mind.

Rule of this game is that each player can move a foot at a time or just jump once. But to eliminate others, the player's foot should touch the to the one they are trying to eliminate. Once this is done, the person who couldn't save themselves moves out of the area.

This starts with a circle. Everyone is holding each other's hands. I have Kinsey on my right and Ethan on my left. Kinsey and I are holding hands like we are never letting go. whereas Ethan gave me his index finger like our parents use to so that we won't be lost when we were small.

I won the first round and now everyone is like

"let's eliminate the birthday girl first."

We played for another hour or so.

"Oh fish! I forgot that Mr. Aden called you." Cyrus says out of blue.

"Time?" I asked, trying not to panic.

"Now is the time." he motions towards the door. "He might be in the staff room" he adds and I sprint to the admin area.

Why would Mr. Aden call *me* on a Saturday afternoon to the staff room? Have I done something wrong?

Everyone followed me to the staff room and it turns out he called everyone but Cyrus wanted me to panic on purpose. That is why he told me that Mr. Aden was especially asking for me.

Mr. Aden gave each one of us our topics for summer vacation project. "Complete this before getting back and I won't tolerate any of you getting late after the vacation get over. *Only if you are coming back*" he gave us some instructions and added the last part looking at me as if it's an indirect question to me.

"Off course I am coming back." I lied.

"*Off course*" he repeated like he caught me.

I went to the operators' room which is just beside the staffroom just to make sure when my parents were going to arrive. The lady sitting there called my mom to check.

"They just arrived at the main gate," she told me once she hung up. "And you have to pick your extra luggage from the dining hall area." she added.

I am speechless.

It's hard for me to digest that my journey here has come to an end.

No... no no no nonononono not now.

Not this soon. I was just starting to adjust, to enjoy, to accept.

Before I realise, I am running towards the dining area. When I'm there, a van is standing there in the parking lot and my suitcase is kept beside it. I had a ton of stuff and the luggage I already had was not enough to fit everything so, I asked my parents to bring an extra one. Now that I have collected it and reached the hostel, I am trying to adjust whatever I can in this.

Kinsey triggers me by saying something she shouldn't have. Now I am throwing things.

Everywhere.

I am screaming at her.

My heart going to explode out of my ribcage.

Another word out of my mouth would make droplets of tears held back in her eyes burst out.

I am looking at other five people who are in my room staring at me like I am mad.

I am going mad.

And last but not the least,

I cry.

I grabbed Kinsey's wrist and dragged her out of the room. We both hugged each other like never before and we cried together.

I have a total of eighteen bags which the driver is trying to fit in the van. It took me around 2 hours to pack my homeless/bag-less belongings. Kinsey sat with me in the van and I asked the driver to take a halt in the dining area. I ran towards the computer lab which is in front of the dining hall and I could spot Ethan.

I have no idea why I expected everyone to be here.

"You are coming with me, right? To get your stuff" I asked Ethan.

"I went there as soon as you received the call but, the security didn't allow your parents to bring anything." He gave me a sad smile. One I could rarely see.

Why was I even expecting that we will be able to fool them?

Ethan and I shook hands and then he asked me

"You are not coming next year, right?" He knew the answer to his question, he asked me just to be sure.

I didn't tell anyone about this.

How does he know? I guess he noticed me acting weird when everyone was discussing next year. Not only him but Trevor and Cyrus also noticed something but they never tried to ask me.

WHY did he ask it now of all time?

I wanted to say to him that he is the biggest jerk I have ever met but, he wasn't that bad. I wanted to thank everyone that even after being such crazy idiots, they were the people I felt comfortably attached with. All of them were the core part of my time spent here and memories made here. Before I could say anything,

My hands went numb...

My legs were hurting from the rush...

My shoulders feel heavy...

I say ye—

My head is already hurting from the impending trauma,

I gave him a small nod.

My vision blurred,

I turned.

Epilogue

Strangers

No, we are not enemies

No, we are not lovers

No, we are not friends

Yes, we are strangers

Strangers with common thoughts

Strangers with same memories

Strangers who know everything about each other, yet strangers

Strangers who talk to each other after swearing on breaking contact

Strangers who mock each other

Strangers who discuss present, hate the past, and predict the future

Just strangers with some strange connection

Once friends, forever strangers

Acknowledgements

I never thought I would be writing a book at this age. My life has so much drama and plot twists that I could make a series and that's what my father suggested me.

Thank you for being the biggest supporter. It was his idea that I could preserve my creative mind. He worked hard and enlightened me in every aspect of my life.

My mother made sure my healthy appetite and provided me with different source of self-improvement. Thankyou Mumma and Papa.

Both my parents are my heroes. Words aren't enough for them. Moreover, my grandparents took a very good care of me while I was working on my last part of this book, I was staying at their place for a while when my parents were not around. They allowed me to share my ideas with them and helped me keeping myself fit.

My elder brother has always been my best friend. I have always shared all my secrets with him and he help me process though my fears. We do fight sometimes like every other sibling but having this bond with him is a blessing to me. Thank you for allowing me to tell you everything and helping me out of the mess I created every time.

I always wanted to do something like this for which my Nanu would feel proud. He was one of the most brilliant and jolly natured people I have ever known. Thank you for always encouraging me.

Lastly, I would like to thank the person who is always there to remind me of the best memories I have created with her. No matter how much we fought, she never left my side. Thanks to you that you kept reminding me the important bits I forgot every time.

I would like to thank my every supporter and everyone who appreciated me throughout this journey. People who gave me hope, never left my side.

I would like to acknowledge my publishing team for helping me by giving a proper source to bring my creativity to the world, looking forward to work with you.

Special thanks to Lucy, thanks for existing and keeping me company.

About the Author

Overthinking can be a good sign,
I get a ton of thoughts late nights

I think I should shut down my mind,
But my processor keeps pushing forward and rewind

Why am I so active on social sites?
Being an introvert all the time

I can be anything but stay quiet,
Always regretting my choice of line

No, these are not just poem lines
These describe my real life

I am Olivia Bell, a teenager who started her journey in a small town. I have attended four different school with more than forty different experiences and that's what motivated me to write. I am so influenced by the fictional world that I am starting to create one for my own.

www.ingramcontent.com/pod-product-compliance
Lightning Source LLC
LaVergne TN
LVHW041938070526
838199LV00051BA/2836